Top Wing...

Top Wing • • • • • •

by Matt Christopher

Illustrated by Marcy Ramsey

 Little, Brown and Company
Boston   New York   Toronto   London

To C. Christopher, Kimberly, and Samantha Jo

Text copyright © 1994 by Matthew F. Christopher
Illustrations copyright © 1994 by Marcy Ramsey

First Paperback Edition

Library of Congress Cataloging-in-Publication Data
Christopher, Matt.
    Top wing / Matt Christopher. — 1st ed.
        p.   cm.
    Summary: Dana Bellamy searches for the truth behind the fire for which his father is being blamed.
    ISBN 0-316-14099-6 (hc)
    ISBN 0-316-14126-7 (pb)
[1. Mystery and detective stories.   2. Soccer — Fiction.]
I. Title.
PZ7.C458Tn   1994
[Fic] — dc20   93-5218

10   9   8   7   6   5   4   3   2   1
MV-NY

Published simultaneously in Canada
by Little, Brown & Company (Canada) Limited

Printed in the United States of America

Top Wing • • •

1 • • •

"It's going, going . . ."

"It looks like it's in there . . ."

"Goal!"

Dana Bellamy could almost see the imaginary soccer ball sailing across the goal line and into the net. He turned to his friends Steve Rapids and Benton Crawford, and grinned.

The three friends raised their fists in victory — even though it wasn't a real one.

As they walked home together, they relived the winning goal that Steve, the center forward for the Anchors, had put by the opposing goalie during soccer practice.

"Boy, I wish that had been a real game," said Dana. The twelve-year-old right wing for the Anchors slapped his teammate on the back. "Great kick, Steve," he said.

Benton echoed Dana's praise. "Way to go," he said. "Gotta make a few like that when we play tomorrow."

"Ol' Steve here's going to lead us on to victory," said Dana. "How's it feel to be captain?"

"No one's ever going to replace Shins Sullivan," said Steve. The longtime Anchors captain had recently moved out of state. After practice that afternoon, following Steve's spectacular goal, the team had elected him to the leadership spot.

"Yeah, but you're the best player on the team," said Dana.

"Not the strongest, though," Benton added, darting between the others as he dribbled an invisible soccer ball down the street. He stopped a few yards in front of them as a fit of coughing overtook him.

"Course not," said Steve, thumping Benton on the back. "Everyone knows Abe Strom's the team gorilla. And you're our power halfback!"

"Yeah, but I think Abe thought that he should be the new captain," said Benton, still coughing slightly as he hiked up his schoolbooks under his arm.

"You're right, Bent," said Dana. "I think he was a little disappointed."

"What the heck," said Benton. "He'll get over it."

"Maybe I ought to talk to him," said Steve. "For the good of the team. I mean, we have to put that ahead of everything."

"Better believe it," said Dana.

They had reached the corner of the street where Dana and Benton lived.

Dana nodded in the direction of his house. "You guys want to come in? We can see if there's a game on the sports channel."

"No, thanks," said Steve. "I promised my dad I'd clean up some junk in the garage. I better get that done."

"What about you, Bent? Want to see if there are any of my mom's killer brownies left?"

"Nah, I have to get home, too," said Benton. "My folks are going to a wedding."

"Tonight?" asked Dana.

"Yup," Benton answered. "Mom said something

about a sunset ceremony, so I'd better get a move on. Besides, I want to hole up in my secret hiding place and finish reading that new dinosaur book."

"Well, see you guys tomorrow," said Steve.

"See you," called Benton and Dana as they started to jog down their street together. It was too short a distance for a real race, but by mutual agreement, they always put on some speed as they passed the fireplug fifty yards away from the Crawfords' driveway.

Benton waved back at Dana as he swung into the driveway and went in the back door of his house.

Dana was lying on the floor listening to the stereo. But something was wrong with the CD, because the same note was repeating over and over. It kept blaring and blaring and blaring.

Dana woke up suddenly. It wasn't music — it was a fire alarm!

The house is on fire! Dana thought wildly. But as he sat up in bed, he realized the sound was coming from outside the house. Besides, he thought, that's not the sound our smoke detectors make.

A strange bright light shone in through his bedroom window. He jumped out of bed and looked outside.

"Holy cow!" he gasped. Orange and yellow flames were streaming out of the windows of the Crawford house. Thick black smoke poured out around them. "The Crawfords' house is on fire!"

Dana grabbed his jacket and threw it on over his pajamas. He raced downstairs and almost crashed into his parents outside the front door. His little sister, Christy, was right behind him.

"What's happening?" he asked.

"Your father smelled the smoke and woke up," said Mrs. Bellamy. "He rang the alarm on the pole across the street."

"Have you seen Benton and Letitia?" Dana asked in a panic. "They're all by themselves in there!"

"What?" cried Mr. Bellamy. "Bill Crawford's car isn't in the driveway. I thought they were all away somewhere this evening."

"Mr. and Mrs. Crawford went to a wedding," Dana blurted out.

"And didn't ask us to keep an eye on the kids? Oh, my goodness," Mrs. Bellamy cried. "Those children really might be in there, then. I'm calling 911 and telling them to send an ambulance right away." She dashed off to make the call.

Mr. Bellamy had already stepped inside and grabbed his gardening boots from the closet. He shoved his bare feet inside them and threw on a heavy jacket.

"What are you doing, Dad?" Dana asked.

"I have to see if those kids are in there," Mr. Bellamy called back as he ran over to the burning house. "There's a chance I can still get them out safely."

"But, Dad —," Dana called after him. He wanted to go with him, to help. But he knew he should stay out of the way and keep an eye on Christy.

By this time, people from other houses in the neighborhood had heard the alarm, too, and had gathered nearby.

Mrs. Bellamy, clutching the cordless telephone, had come back outside.

"Where's your father?" she asked.

"He's gone to find Benton and Letitia."

"Where?"

"Inside the house," said Dana, tugging at her bathrobe sleeve. He pulled her along with him across their driveway toward the burning building.

Far off in the distance, Dana could hear the sound of fire engines. Why can't they hurry and get here faster? he thought.

The smell of smoke was getting stronger outside the Crawford house. The flames licked higher and higher.

"I can't believe he's in there." Mrs. Bellamy's voice was thick with anxiety. "Are you sure he went inside?"

"I saw him. He went right in," said Dana. He stared at the front of the Crawford house. Suddenly he saw a movement. "Wait a minute! He's coming out! Dad!"

"He's carrying someone!" cried Mrs. Bellamy.

Sure enough, Mr. Bellamy came through the

front door with a huddled form in his arms. Several people in the crowd rushed forward to help relieve him of his burden. Dana looked over and saw Benton Crawford sprawled out on the ground. He was coughing and sputtering, but he looked unharmed.

Dana rushed over to see if he could do anything to help his friend.

Mrs. Bellamy ran toward her husband. But before she could reach him, he rushed back into the house.

"What's he going back in there for?" someone in the crowd yelled out.

"He's crazy! It's an inferno!" someone else shouted.

"Letitia!" cried Mrs. Bellamy. "He's gone back for Letitia!"

Seconds turned into minutes that seemed like hours as the house continued to burn. There was no sign of any movement at all. The flames continued to blaze away.

With their sirens wailing, several fire trucks came speeding around the corner and pulled up in front of the Crawford house. A few fire fighters grabbed the hose and ran down to connect it to the hydrant.

Dana was so busy watching the fire fighters, he almost didn't notice when the little girl came running out of the house.

"Mom! Look!" he cried.

It was Letitia, all by herself.

Mrs. Bellamy caught the little girl.

"Letitia! Where's Mr. Bellamy? What happened?" she asked.

"I don't know," said Letitia, sobbing. "He was carrying me and . . . and then he dropped me. I fell. And then I just ran toward the front door!"

One of the firemen must have heard what she said, because he called back to the others, "There's still someone in there! Let's go!"

The hose was turned on. A squad of fire fighters wearing protective masks and suits grabbed their equipment. They forced their way through the smoke belching out the windows and door and entered the house.

Dana could feel the heat from the fire on his

face. Then, through the noise of the crowd and the sound of the fire's destruction, he heard a shout.

"We've got him!"

He clutched his mother's arm and held his breath. Would his dad be all right? Would he be alive?

Two firemen stumbled out the front door. They gently laid Mr. Bellamy's limp form on the ground. Mrs. Bellamy, Dana, and Christy rushed toward him. Dana heard another siren coming closer and closer.

"That's an ambulance," said one of the firemen. "How'd they get here so fast?"

"I dialed 911 when I heard the children were trapped inside," said Mrs. Bellamy. She held Mr. Bellamy's hand and leaned down over him.

His eyes were shut, but he was breathing. Every now and then, he coughed violently.

"Better move back and let the EMTs take over," said the fire chief.

"Dad!" shouted Dana. "Are you okay?"

"What happened? Why isn't he speaking?" asked Mrs. Bellamy.

"We found him under a heap of rubble," said one of the firemen. "Don't know what fell on him or how much damage it did."

"But he's alive," said another fireman. "And lucky at that."

The ambulance pulled up next to the fire trucks. Three EMTs jumped out and went right to work. They eased a stretcher under Mr. Bellamy and lifted him into the back of the ambulance.

Mrs. Bellamy climbed in after him.

"I'm going with them," she said. "Dana, you stay here and look after your sister."

"We'll take care of them," said one of their neighbors. "Don't worry."

Don't worry? As the ambulance sped off into the night, Dana knew that worrying was exactly what he would be doing — worrying and wondering if his father would come through.

2 • • •

The Hammerville Herald

Good Samaritan Hospitalized

Man Stricken Saving Neighbors' Two Children in House Fire

HAMMERVILLE: Hayden Bellamy, 41, of 2012 Lotus Street, suffered severe smoke inhalation while rescuing his neighbors' two children from a near-fatal fire that began at approximately ten o'clock last night.

Martin and Grace Crawford were attending a friend's wedding reception when the fire, which started from an undetermined source, began. It was already raging beyond control when Bellamy, alerted by the smell of smoke, arrived at the scene.

He rushed in and rescued the boy, whose bedroom

is closest to the front of the house. While in the process of rescuing the girl, he was struck from behind by a piece of debris and fell, knocking his head against a door casing. But the girl could see the open doorway ahead and managed to run for her life from the house.

Fire fighters on the scene were able to remove Bellamy from the burning building. After they had applied cardiopulmonary resuscitation, Bellamy was rushed to Hammerville General Hospital, where he is listed in serious condition.

No matter how many times he read the newspaper article, Dana could scarcely believe that the fire had happened.

Mr. Bellamy was in the intensive care ward of the hospital. There was a tube stuck into his arm to give him food and nourishment. Another tube went up his nose and down his throat. But he was gaining strength. All the doctors and nurses said his chances of recovering were good. Everyone just had to be patient, they said.

"I'm telling you, Dana," said Mrs. Bellamy, putting on her coat. "There's nothing you can do at the hospital. And you know they only let you see him for a few minutes at a time."

Dana shook his head. "I still don't know if I should play in today's game."

"There's absolutely no reason not to," Mrs. Bellamy insisted. "This is the first nice day since that awful hot spell. Two horrible, steamy weeks of it! Thank goodness for fans and air conditioners. Now, have some fun, Dana. Let's get in the car. Come on, Christy — you, too."

Dana's ten-year-old sister hopped into the backseat of the station wagon.

"I'll give Dad a big hug for you," said Christy. "And after the game, you can tell him how many goals you made."

All season long, Dana had been one of the top scorers for the Hammerville Anchors, right behind Steve Rapids. But he had skipped the last game, which was right after the fire. This would be his first day back in action.

And the Anchors really needed him. With the season well under way, they were trailing the

Cottoneers in the league standings by two games. A win today would mean a big boost in the Anchors' morale.

Mrs. Bellamy shifted into reverse and backed out of the driveway. Dana saw her glance at the charred remains of the Crawford house.

As she started down the road, Dana noticed Andrea McGowan across the street. The fifteen-year-old redheaded girl was sitting on the top step of her front porch. She held a video camera to her right eye. It was aimed at a large oak tree near the corner of her front yard.

What's so interesting about an oak tree? Dana wondered.

"Oh, look!" Christy exclaimed. "Andrea's making a movie of that squirrel nibbling on an acorn! Isn't that cute!"

Dana grinned. "Yeah," he said. "Real cute."

At that moment, Andrea lowered the camera and waved at the passing car. Andrea was a real video nut. Her favorite way of spending time was making a videotape of just about anything.

Well, almost anything. Dana had once asked her if she'd like to videotape one of his soccer games.

"What?" she'd asked, wrinkling her nose. "Two hours of watching a bunch of kids kicking a ball back and forth? Forget it. Not enough excitement, not enough action."

The car turned the corner, and Andrea's red hair became a dim spark in the distance.

After weaving through the downtown area, Mrs. Bellamy pulled into the parking lot next to the soccer field.

Dana unbuckled his seat belt and jumped out of the car.

"See you after the game," said his mother. "Have fun — and good luck."

"Yeah — good luck," echoed Christy.

"Thanks a bunch," said Dana, giving them the thumbs-up sign.

The car took off, and Dana trotted over to a group of boys warming up near the south goal area. Like them, he wore the Anchors' navy blue uniform with the red trim around the edges and his number in white on the front and back. Dana had chosen number twelve since he'd just celebrated his twelfth birthday.

The Cottoneers were at the opposite side of the

field. Clothed in their yellow uniforms with the green trim, the opposition ran back and forth across the field, keeping a half dozen soccer balls in motion. Coming off a three-game winning streak, they were the favorite — even in enemy territory.

The Anchors' coach, Russ Kingsley, seemed ready for them. Throughout the season, he'd taught the team that a strong offense and a heads-up defense were the keys to winning. He positioned his team in a 3-3-4 lineup. Dana, Steve, and Abe Strom made up the front line, with Dana to Steve's right and Abe at the left wing position. At midfield Coach Kingsley placed Jack Nguyen in the center, flanked by Lance Dixon on his left and Benton on his right. The backfield went from left to right: Tucker Fromm, Paul Crayton, Pete Morris, then Mike Vass. Jazz McCord held down the goalie slot on the team.

The first member of the team to notice Dana's arrival was the new captain of the Anchors.

"Hey, Dana," said Steve. "Glad you could make it."

"Yeah, we were just asking about you," said Jazz. "Weren't sure you'd want to play." He kicked a practice ball over toward Dana.

"How's your dad?" asked Pete, nudging the ball away from him.

"Okay. He's doing okay," Dana answered.

Jack dribbled a ball in Dana's direction, then faked it away from him. He called back as he edged toward the goal area, "I was sorry to hear he got burned."

"It was mostly smoke inhalation," said Dana. "His lungs are in bad shape, but he's coming along. He's getting better."

The ball was booted back and forth, stolen, passed, trapped, and kicked, over and over, as the Anchors shook out the kinks and got ready for the game. During the warm-up, most of the guys managed to say a word or two to Dana about his dad.

As a whistle blew to signal that the game was about to start, both teams ran off to their benches. Dana noticed Benton lagging toward the back of the group. He waved at his neighbor, but Benton had his head down. Dana was anxious to talk to

Benton because they hadn't seen each other much since the fire. The Crawfords were temporarily living across town in an apartment.

"Hey, Bent!" he called over.

But before there was a chance to talk, Coach Kingsley clapped his hands to get the attention of his players. "Okay, you guys," he said. "Gather round! Steve, you know what to say if you win the toss?"

"Kick," answered the tall, broad-shouldered center forward.

"Right," said the coach. "And Dana, you'll take the position inside the circle with him. Remember, Steve, a quick tap to Dana. Dana, you boot it to Benton, run downfield, and look for his pass. Got it?"

Both teams gathered at the center of the field, where the referee and two line judges were waiting. The referee asked the Cottoneer captain, Russ Anderson, to make the call. Then he flipped the coin.

"Heads!" shouted Anderson.

Heads it was. The Cottoneers chose to kick.

The referee looked over at Steve. "Which goal?" he asked.

The Anchors' captain pointed to the south goal.

As the players ran toward their positions, a loud noise burst out behind their bench. Six cheerleaders dressed in the team colors flung their arms in the air and kicked up their legs. They led the Anchors' fans in a loud cheer.

> *Jupiter, Saturn, Venus, Mars,*
> *Have you seen those Anchors stars?*
> *What a sight,*
> *What a treat,*
> *We're the team that can't be beat!*

Meanwhile the teams got set on the field. Dana crouched anxiously in the right wing slot. Adrenaline rushed through his system as he waited for the opening kick.

Seconds later, the ball came zooming across the field. The Cottoneer center had kicked the ball back to his halfback, who had aimed a kick to his right wing. But his kick was off. The ball landed midway between Lance and Abe. Both of them rushed toward it. About half the Cottoneers made for the same spot.

But Lance got to the ball first. He dribbled it a few feet before booting it in Jack's direction.

Jack was in the clear. But in a matter of seconds, there were a half dozen Cottoneers swooping down on him. Dana knew he couldn't stand and wait for the ball to come to him. He rushed over in Jack's direction, looking for a pass.

"Jack! Over here!" he yelled.

Jack managed to get off a pass in his general direction. Dana lined himself up, planted his feet, and trapped the ball with his chest. He let it drop to the ground, then dribbled it toward the touch-line.

Through the sea of yellow-and-green uniforms downfield, he looked for someone in the clear. Where was Abe? Where was Steve?

There was no time to waste. A Cottoneer was all over him. Dana tried to dribble the ball away. He just managed to avoid a steal when another Cottoneer halfback appeared at his side. He had to pass the ball quickly — or have it stolen.

Fortunately Benton was right behind him. Dana wobbled a pass to him seconds before the tackler reached in with his foot. The Cottoneer had simply been too slow.

Benton started to move the ball downfield, toward the Cottoneers' goal. Dana saw him look around. Steve was covered all over like wallpaper by the defense. And Abe was too far off. But Dana had shaken loose and was running just slightly ahead of him. With a little luck, he'd have a clear shot at the goal.

He figured Benton would pass the ball to him automatically. After all, that's part of what halfbacks were supposed to do — get the ball to the front line. And the two of them had been a scoring combination throughout the season.

But Benton kept on dribbling the ball, wasting valuable time.

"Benton! Bent!" he shouted. "Over here!"

It was too late. A bunch of Cottoneers had caught up with the Anchors' midfielder. In a last-ditch effort to save the ball from a steal, Benton kicked it toward the sideline. It ricocheted off a Cottoneer and was about to go out of bounds. At the last second, Mike Vass made a run for it, but it bounced off his shin and over the line.

The whistle blew.

"Green ball!" shouted the ref.

As the two teams lined up for the throw-in, Dana glanced over at Benton. He was about to shrug and signal "Better luck next time." But he just couldn't seem to catch Benton's eye.

3 • • •

When the ball came into play, it was headed in Jack Nguyen's direction. The Anchors' center half-back snagged the ball between his shins, then passed it up to Abe Strom in the left wing position.

The ball remained on the left side of the field, bouncing back and forth between the two teams' offense and defense. For a moment, Dana had a chance to catch his breath. He noticed that Benton, several feet behind him, was coughing and gasping. Probably still has some smoke in his lungs, like Dad, Dana thought.

Most of the time, he was able to put the fire out of his mind. But every now and then, it would creep back. When he thought of his father, trapped inside the Crawfords' house, his mouth got dry. And then there had been the long wait until his mother called from the hospital to say that Mr. Bellamy was going to be okay. He couldn't help thinking about that awful time.

Dana shook his head. Not now, he thought. I have to keep my mind on the game and my eye on the ball.

The Anchors' offense had broken away from the cluster of Cottoneers and had crossed the midfield stripe. The ball was about twenty yards in front of the goal line. Steve tried to set up a kick, but he couldn't shake off a Cottoneer defenseman. He tried to boot it toward Dana, but it wobbled back toward Benton instead.

There were too many players from both teams between Benton and the goal. He had to pass the ball.

Two Anchors were in good field position for a goal attempt. Dana had jogged downfield but was still only a dozen yards away from Benton. Lance was way across the field.

Benton twisted around and booted the ball over to Lance.

A Cottoneer swung in front of Lance, ready to intercept. But luckily Jack had shaken loose and got in the way. The ball bounced off his hip — in the wrong direction. A strong kick from a Cotton-eer halfback sent it hurtling toward the Anchors' goal. The Cottoneers' offense raced after the ball.

"Eyes up, Jazz!" Dana called as the two teams converged in the goal area. He jogged along beside the touchline in that direction, careful to stay out of the way. He knew that too many players "help-ing" the defense usually ended up causing a foul — or a goal.

I could've had a shot back there, he thought. I wonder why Benton didn't pass the ball to me. Probably just didn't see me.

A shout from the Cottoneers' fans snapped Dana back to the game. He looked up just in time to see Fred Currier, the Cottoneers' right wing, boot one in. The Anchors were now one goal in the hole.

As the two teams got into position for the kick, Steve tried to rally the Anchors.

"Come on, you guys," he said. "Let's get some teamwork going!"

"Yeah," shouted Dana. "Let's go, Anchors!" Fol-lowing Coach Kingsley's instructions before the game, Dana joined Steve in the center circle for the kickoff.

I only hope Benton is ready for the pass, he thought. He seems a little off his game today.

The ref blew his whistle to signal the kickoff. Steve tapped the ball over to Dana. Dana trapped it smoothly, booted it back to Benton, and took off down the wing slot. As he turned to look for the pass back, he saw Benton stop the ball, look up, then begin dribbling it downfield.

Why doesn't he pass it to me like Coach told him to? Dana thought. Then Benton did pass it — to Steve, who almost missed it. Steve shot a surprised look at Dana, then started with the ball toward the Cottoneers' goal.

Dana kept running downfield about ten yards in from the touchline. He kept right up with Steve, who gradually worked the ball toward the goal.

So far, so good. The rest of the team managed to keep most of the Cottoneers out of the way. But one of their bigger players was bearing down on Steve.

The Anchor captain must have seen the enemy approach. He was still too far for a goal kick. Instead, just breaking stride for a moment, he booted the ball over in Dana's direction.

Dana was all clear. There was no one near him, and he had a great shot at the goal. It was a golden opportunity.

Then, out of nowhere, a flash of navy blue with red trim zoomed in between him and the ball. One of his own teammates had stolen the ball!

The shock of jet black hair on a tall, lanky form told him exactly who it was. Benton!

The Anchor halfback was traveling at lightning speed — away from Dana and straight toward the left side of the field. With a quick flick of his foot, he passed the ball to Abe.

Abe dribbled it closer to the goal, just managing to keep it away from two Cottoneers trying to pry it loose. He was within the penalty area when one of the Cottoneers rammed into him from behind and knocked him on his backside.

A whistle shrieked.

"Direct free kick," announced the referee. It was the Anchors' chance to tie the score.

"Make it good, Abe!" Dana called over to him.

"You can do it!" echoed Steve.

Abe didn't even look at them. He got up and brushed the back of his shorts. Then, from the spot where he'd been hit, he kicked the ball toward the goal.

His aim was off. The ball hit a goalpost and rebounded in an arc over Dana's head.

Dana turned to see if Benton was in position to stop the ball from traveling far upfield. With a thud, it landed directly in front of the right half-back. All he had to do was dribble it to one side and he'd be in a good position to pass.

But Benton had turned away from the action. It looked as though he was coughing. The ball went right by him. Fortunately Jack was close enough to make a lunge for it. He scooped it away before the Cottoneers could claim it.

"Jack!" called Dana. "Jack, on your right!"

Dana could see a couple of Cottoneer uniforms closing in on the Anchor halfback. Benton was nearby, though, and managed to grab on to a short pass with the instep of his left foot. He dribbled the ball downfield, looking for a teammate in the clear.

Once again, Dana was the logical choice. And

once again, Benton went his own way. Only this time, he had barely moved when a Cottoneer tackler got in the way. In no time at all, the ball was skyrocketing back toward the Anchors' goal.

Dana was about to shout at Benton when he saw him lean over, hands on his knees, panting for breath.

The first half's not even over, and he's already winded, Dana thought. He'll never make it through the game.

There was no time to worry about Benton. The ball was loose at midfield. There was a wild scramble. The same tackler who'd stolen it from Benton had it now. He was getting set for a pass to one of the Cottoneer wings.

Dana made his move. He rushed right into the ball's path and caught it smack on the side of his head. It hit him so hard, he was stunned for a second. When his head cleared, he saw that his block hadn't done much good. The impact had knocked it out of bounds.

The Cottoneer halfback threw the ball in from the sideline. One of the biggest guys in a green-and-yellow uniform wrenched it loose from the tangle of stabbing legs and booted it toward the Anchors' goal.

But Jazz was on his toes. He caught the ball in midair and quickly put it back into play, aiming it for Abe.

The Anchors' left wing was a little slow getting to the ball. A Cottoneer intercepted and sent the ball back toward the goal. It got as far as the penalty area, where fullback Tucker Fromm went after it. There was a race between him and the Cottoneers' speedy right wing. They reached the ball at the same time. Each tried to shake it loose, kicking and stumbling in the attempt. Dana could only watch as their arms flapped wildly at their sides and their legs got all tangled up.

For a second, it seemed that Tucker had the upper edge. He had managed to nudge the ball to one side when another Cottoneer cut in and stole it away.

Coach Kingsley was shouting from the Anchors' bench, "Defense! Defense!"

The Cottoneers' coach was yelling, "Kick! Kick!"

Then a whistle blew, and the first half of the game was over.

The Cottoneers had the lead: 1–0.

"Down by one," Dana grumbled out loud as he ran toward the bench. He noticed that Benton, a few feet to one side, was giving him an icy scowl.

"What's that look for?" asked Dana. "It wasn't my fault they scored."

"Lucky they didn't get another," said Abe, coming between the two of them. "You practically gave them the ball with that head block."

"You're nuts!" Dana protested. "It almost took my head off! It's not like I messed up a pass or something!"

"Knock it off, you guys," said the coach. "Gather round."

The Anchors formed a small circle around him. They passed orange slices and water around. The coach let them catch their breath and cool off. Then he spoke up.

"You're playing it too tight," he said. "You're not spreading out and looking for opportunities. 'Heads up' means just that — keeping your eyes open. And working together. You have to start acting like a team. Got that?"

"Got it!"

"Rah!"

"Go, Anchors!"

The cheers rang out as the second half began.

Within a few seconds of play, the Anchors had moved the ball deep into Cottoneer territory. Abe, Steve, and Dana passed the ball among themselves, looking for an opening.

For a minute, it looked like Steve would get a chance to score. But a fast-moving Cottoneer made a move between him and the goal, blocking his path. Another defenseman worked his way over and wriggled the ball away. A quick kick started the ball back upfield toward the Anchors' goal.

"Behind you, Dana! Behind you!"

He whirled around as Steve's voice broke through. The ball had ricocheted off a Cottoneer and was sizzling on the ground toward him. It was going so fast, he barely was able to stop it. But he stuck out his foot, blocked the ball, then spun around toward the goal.

Two fullbacks in green and yellow came charging toward him. He had to move fast. He spotted Steve darting toward the goal.

Dribbling the ball to his left, he suddenly shifted his position and booted the ball over toward the middle of the field.

Steve was waiting for it. He trapped it with the inside of his left foot and began to dribble it toward the goal.

But two Cottoneers were in the way. They charged at him from opposite directions.

Abe tried to help out, but he was trapped. Dana was closer to Steve than any of the other Anchors. He made for the right side of the goal and yelled, "Steve!"

The Anchor captain squeezed out a pass in his direction. Dana ran straight at it and booted it toward the goal. He hoped it would get by an open space to the left, beyond the reach of the Cottoneer goalie.

The ball just missed.

It struck a goalpost and bounced off to the left side of the field, way out of play.

Dana's heart sank.

He couldn't remember when missing a goal had felt so bad.

4 • • •

Down in front of the stands, the Anchors' cheer-leaders did their best to lift the team's spirits.

> *Come on Anchors,*
> *Really dig in,*
> *Show 'em you're the team*
> *That's going to win!*

> *Anchors! Anchors!*
> *Sis! Boom! Bah!*
> *Anchors! Anchors!*
> *Hip! Hip! Hoorah!*

As play continued, Dana didn't feel much like cheering. But he couldn't give up now. There was too much at stake.

The Cottoneers controlled the ball for a long

time without scoring. For a while it looked as though the Anchors' defense would wear them down. Anchors fullback Paul Crayton, who hadn't seen much action in the first half, had come alive. It seemed as though he was everywhere now.

"Way to go, Paul!" Dana called after a good block, which gave the Anchors control of the ball. Paul booted it out of the penalty area.

Dana made a move for it, but Steve got there ahead of him. At least part of him did. The ball bounced off his right hip and rolled over toward Dana.

By now, the Cottoneers were beginning to advance toward the Anchors' right wing. He saw he wasn't going to move very far with the ball. Looking around, he saw Benton, all by himself, down in the penalty area.

Dana knew he should pass it to him. An assist that resulted in a goal was almost as good as a score. But the memory of Benton stealing the ball from him earlier made him hesitate.

He waited one second too long. In that time, Cottoneers were all over Benton and the coast was no longer clear. Instead, Dana passed the ball to

Jack, who came running up beside him, one step ahead of a Cottoneer tackler. Jack trapped the ball with his instep, then passed it right back to him.

Dana was surprised by the quick return, but he took the ball, dribbled it a few feet, then got it within kicking distance of the goal — while a Cottoneer tackler was breathing down his neck. Suddenly their legs got tangled up with each other. The tackler fell and the whistle shrieked.

"Tripping!" yelled the referee. Dana saw him pointing a stiff finger in his direction.

He couldn't believe it. The Cottoneer was as much at fault as he was! Still, he knew you couldn't argue with a referee and win. He shook his head but kept his mouth shut.

A free kick was called. Because the foul had occurred within the defending team's penalty area, all players had to be outside the area. Dana tried to guess where the Cottoneer would aim his kick and positioned himself nearby.

Well, at least I didn't cost the team a goal, Dana said to himself, eyes on his opponent.

He spoke too soon. The Cottoneer booted the ball to a teammate centerfield. The receiving player didn't waste any time booting it even farther downfield toward the Anchors' territory.

The Cottoneers' speedy center got behind the ball and dribbled quickly toward the goal. He faked around Pete Morris into the penalty area. Jazz shifted back and forth, arms spread wide, but the lanky center was too quick for him. A sharp kick sent the ball straight into the net.

Cottoneers 2, Anchors 0.

"Teamwork! Teamwork!" shouted Coach Kingsley from the bench.

There didn't seem to be a lot of that happening on the Anchors' side of the field.

"Okay, guys, heads up!" shouted Dana as the ball came into play.

For a few minutes, it looked as though the tide might turn. Jack got the ball and dribbled it toward the goal. When the Cottoneers closed in on him, he passed it to Lance.

Lance did some fancy footwork and kept the ball moving in the right direction. When he got into trouble, he passed it across the field to Benton.

Benton brought the ball well within scoring range, but couldn't seem to find an opening for a goal attempt. Dana tried to get his attention, but he couldn't catch Benton's eye. Instead, Benton booted the ball over to Steve.

Who could argue with that? Steve was the best goal kicker on the team, after all.

But Steve was also a real team player. Dana could see that there wasn't an opening between Steve and the goal. Sure enough, Steve kept it moving, passing it to Jack. Jack tried to get off a kick toward the goal, but the ball got into a tangle of Cottoneer defensemen. When it bobbled free, it was right in front of Dana.

The Anchors' right wing didn't hesitate. He booted it. Hard.

Goal!

A cheer went up from the stands.

The scoreboard now read Cottoneers 2, Anchors 1.

But the clock was still running. There was no time to waste on congratulations if the Anchors were going to win.

They hurried upfield to get ready for the kick. As Dana jogged by Benton to get into position, Benton suddenly doubled over in a fit of coughing.

Concerned, Dana stopped and thumped Benton lightly on the back.

"Hey, are you okay?" he said.

Benton shook off Dana's arm abruptly and stood up. He glared at Dana and sneered, "Lot you care!" Then he stalked off to his place on the field.

Stunned, Dana almost didn't hear the ref's whistle signaling the kickoff. Then he didn't have time to think because the ball was in play.

The kick was short but high in the air. It landed smack in the middle of the Cottoneers' forward line. They were so set to rush forward, it took them by surprise. That gave the Anchors a chance to press their defense.

The ball rolled around, booted and bumped by several players before Lance got hold of it. He had stayed away from the scramble and had been in the clear.

Lance dribbled it toward the Cottoneers' goal for a few feet before passing it to Jack.

But Jack didn't get far with it before a Cottoneer halfback moved in on him.

Dana had run down beside Jack and was open on his right side.

"Over here!" called Dana.

By now, two more Cottoneers were approaching Jack. The Anchor midfielder had to get rid of the ball. He passed it over to Dana on his right side.

The pass was high. Dana trapped it with his chest. He let it drop to his feet, then dribbled it away from the swarm in the middle of the field.

He was a few feet in from the touchline, looking around for an open Anchor receiver downfield.

From the corner of his left eye, he saw a Cottoneer come sweeping toward him with determination. Dana could almost hear the enemy's thoughts: Nothing was going to stop him from stealing the ball!

The Anchor wing swiveled to avoid the steal — but another Cottoneer appeared out of nowhere between him and the touchline. A fast-moving foot in a green stocking snagged the ball away. The happy Cottoneer then booted it in the other direction, toward the Anchors' goal.

But the ball didn't get more than five feet before Benton was on top of it. He trapped it with the inside of his left foot.

Benton couldn't move with it. A Cottoneer lurking to his blind side rushed over and went for the ball.

"Bent! Here!" Dana shouted.

The distance between them was just about ten feet — and it was clear now.

Dana waved furiously. All Benton had to do was boot the ball to him. He had a good chance to send it way down toward the goal.

And time was running out.

But Benton acted as though he hadn't even heard Dana. He passed the ball in the other direction.

Abe was the only one of the Anchors with a chance to grab it. He nearly had it when a Cottoneer rushed in front of him. The ball bounced off the defender's thigh and hurtled toward Tucker.

There was a hurried scramble for the ball. So many players were all over each other, Dana expected to hear a penalty called any second.

But the Cottoneer offense managed to shake it loose and move it toward the Anchors' goal.

Once again, the Anchors' defense had to dig in.

They did their best and ended up blocking two goal kicks from the penalty area. But Cottoneer captain Russ Anderson couldn't be kept down. Time and again he broke away from the pack. He was all by himself, just ten yards from the goal line when the ball was passed to him.

It looked as though there was no way to keep him from scoring this time.

He booted the ball toward an open space to Jazz's right.

Jazz made a flying leap in the direction of the oncoming ball. At the last second, he tipped it with an open palm.

The impact was enough to knock the ball forward. It bounced just far enough for Steve to snag it. He dribbled off to one side as a cheer was heard from the stands.

"A locomotive for Jazz!" cried one of the cheerleaders.

> *Give me some steam!*
> *Give me some heat!*
> *We're the team that can't be beat!*

Rah! Rah! Rah!
Jazz! Jazz! Jazz!
Go, Anchors, go!

Before Steve could make any headway toward the goal, a whistle shrieked.

It signaled the end of the game.

The Anchors had lost, 2–1.

Benton was only a few feet away from Dana when the whistle blew. But instead of running off the field alongside Dana as he usually did, he called out to Abe and Lance to wait for him.

Dana stopped in his tracks. Then he decided to put his cards right out on the table. He turned back to Benton and called over to him.

"Hey, Bent," he said, "what's going on? Is something eating you? You're acting as though I don't exist or something. You haven't said a single word to me since I showed up today. And you had lots of chances to pass to me, but it was like I was invisible. What's the matter?"

Benton glanced at him quickly. Then he looked away and muttered, "Nothing."

"Nothing? What do you mean?"

"Look, quit bugging me, okay?"

"No, it's not okay," Dana said. "It's messing everything up. We're supposed to be friends as well as teammates. You act like I'm from outer space, like I did something."

"Get off my back," snarled Benton.

Dana was too shocked at Benton's angry tone to reply. As he stood there with his mouth agape, Benton rushed by him toward the bench. He grabbed a paper cup full of water and gulped it down.

Dana recovered his senses and ran over to him. Benton moved away, but Dana grabbed his sleeve.

"What is this, 'Get off my back' baloney?" he demanded. "I thought we were friends. Is that how you think friends should act?"

"No! I think friends are supposed to . . . to watch out for each other," snapped Benton.

"Right! So do I," said Dana. "So when haven't I watched out for you?" He waited for Benton to tell him about some playing mistake he'd made.

"You never told your folks about the wedding!" Benton shouted at him.

"But —," Dana began.

"They should've looked in on us. If they had checked earlier, the fire wouldn't have gotten out of control and our house wouldn't have burned down. So there!"

He threw down the empty paper cup and ran off to join Abe and Lance.

Dana stood there. He was rooted to the ground, his mouth open in amazement.

5 • • •

Dana felt as if he'd been hit in the gut with a ball coming at him at a hundred miles an hour.

Benton couldn't have said what he'd just said!

Benton had never asked him to tell . . . that is, Mr. and Mrs. Crawford never said . . . or Benton never said they'd said —

Wait a minute, he thought. Mom was surprised when I mentioned the wedding the night of the fire. The Crawfords must have forgotten to tell them — and Benton didn't know that. He had it all wrong.

"I'll straighten him out," Dana said out loud.

There was no one around to hear him. Both teams had cleared off the field. There was no one to talk with as he waited in the parking area for his mom to get back. So he had plenty of time to think about what Benton had said.

When Mrs. Bellamy finally arrived, he could hardly wait to get into the car. He wanted to ask her if the Crawfords had mentioned that they were going out the night the fire happened.

But Dana's mom was so excited, he didn't even tell her about the game. She drove down Main Street as fast as the traffic — and the speed limit — would allow as she bubbled over with news.

"You'll never guess what happened," she began.

"Let me! Let me tell!" said Christy. "We didn't see Dad!"

"That's *good* news?" Dana asked.

"It *is!*" said Mrs. Bellamy. "We weren't allowed to see him because he was being examined by the doctors. They decided his condition has improved so much that he's ready for the next step."

"Great!" said Dana. He smiled for the first time in what seemed like hours. "What's the next step?"

"Christy, button your lip," cautioned Mrs. Bellamy. "You'll see when we get there."

Inside the hospital, they took the elevator. Dana

automatically reached for the top floor button. That was where the intensive care section was located.

"Press five," said Mrs. Bellamy. But Christy had already wedged her hand under Dana's. Her pink forefinger pushed the white plastic button. The elevator doors closed and up they went.

They got off on the fifth floor. There Dana discovered that his father had been moved into a private room.

As soon as he got inside, he saw that the tube that went up Mr. Bellamy's nose and down his throat was gone. But the clear plastic bag of colorless liquid was still connected to his arm by an intravenous tube that disappeared under a bandage on his wrist.

Mr. Bellamy was sitting up in bed, all smiles.

After his dad had greeted each of them, Dana asked, "When are they going to take that thing away?" He pointed at the IV tube.

"Pretty soon," said his father. "But it doesn't feel so bad. Hardly even notice it." His voice was a little hoarse.

"I bet you don't miss the nose tube," said Christy.

"I used to think of it as the *throat* tube," said Mr. Bellamy. "I could hardly talk with that thing rubbing away."

That's probably why his voice still sounds kind of raw, thought Dana.

"But I sure heard everything going on," Mr. Bellamy said. He looked over at Dana. "Well, what's the news from the soccer field? Who won the game?"

"Cottoneers," said Dana.

"Score?"

"Two to one."

"It could have been worse," said his father. "How'd you do?"

"I scored the only goal," Dana said.

"Hooray for Dana!" shouted Christy.

"Quiet, dear," said Mrs. Bellamy. "We're in a hospital. Oh, Dana, I'm so glad to hear you made a goal."

"Nice going, son," said Mr. Bellamy. His voice was full of pride. "Did the other team play a lot better? Who had control of the ball most of the time?"

Before Dana could answer, there was a light tapping on the door.

Dr. Higgins, his father's doctor, strode into the room. He was followed by Mrs. Phillips, the head nurse of the fifth floor.

"No need to leave, folks," said Dr. Higgins. He walked over to the bedside. Beneath his curly gray hair and wire-rimmed glasses, he had a friendly smile.

Mrs. Phillips popped a thermometer into Mr. Bellamy's mouth. She picked up his unbandaged hand and checked his pulse. Dr. Higgins, meanwhile, scribbled some notes in a file with Mr. Bellamy's name on it.

The doctor's attention suddenly focused on Dana's uniform.

" 'Anchors,' " he read. "So, you play soccer?"

Dana grinned and nodded.

"Good for you," said Dr. Higgins. "Excellent exercise for the heart and lungs. Make sure you eat properly. Get enough rest and, well, I don't have to tell an athlete like you, no smoking. Right?"

"Right!" Dana agreed quickly.

"Pulse and temperature normal," Mrs. Phillips announced.

"Quite an improvement," said the doctor. "You should be ready to go home in a few days, Hayden. But you still need a lot of rest. This is the best place for you right now."

"If you say so, I'll take your word for it," said Mr. Bellamy. "But when can I start eating real food? Feels like I've lost fifty pounds."

"Oh, I guess they forgot to put the mashed potatoes in that IV," the doctor said, joking. "Seriously, don't be in such a hurry. You'll be back on solid food soon enough. Remember, you had a real close call. If you weren't in such good shape, you might not have made it." He turned to Dana and his family. "But even as strong as he is, I'll bet he could use some sleep. Any excitement could cause a relapse."

You might not have made it. A relapse. The words burned themselves in Dana's head. And if I'm upset thinking about the fire, he thought, imagine how Dad must feel. While the doctor had been doing his examination, Dana had wondered about even mentioning the fire to Mr. Bellamy. Now he knew he had to keep his mouth shut about the night of the fire — and what had happened earlier that day.

The doctor talked with Mrs. Bellamy for a few minutes just outside the door.

She came back into the room and announced, "Dr. Higgins said that you deserve a gold star."

A star. That reminded Dana of the ball hitting him on the head during the game. He smiled and rubbed his head.

"Speaking of stars," Dana said. "I almost saw a few in the game today."

He told them about the ball hitting his head, making it sound funnier than it was. At least Christy laughed a lot.

Mrs. Bellamy warned him to be careful.

"Right," said Mr. Bellamy. "Stay as far away from the ball as possible."

"What?" cried Dana. He knew his father was kidding. "How am I going to be the top scorer that way?"

"Guess you'd better use your head, after all," Mr. Bellamy admitted, yawning.

He was getting tired. It was time to leave.

Christy piped up, "I'm hungry."

Good old Christy, thought Dana.

"I've been thinking about food, too," said Mrs. Bellamy. "Ever since Dr. Higgins mentioned mashed potatoes. Oh, Hayden, maybe I shouldn't have said that!"

"No, that's okay," he said. "You can't be worrying about everything you say. Besides, I can always dream about real food."

"Good, get some rest," said Mrs. Bellamy. "Come on, kids, give him a kiss, and let's go."

"See you tomorrow, Dad," said Dana, kissing his father on the cheek.

He had to hold back the tears that started to well up. His dad's close call still shook him up. So what if he was stuck in the hospital for a few more days? Pretty soon he'd be back home. Everything would be okay again.

Or would it? How would his folks feel when they found out what Benton had said? He had to tell them sometime. They had to clear things up.

As they drove away from the hospital, Christy chattered away. She was obviously glad to see her dad getting better.

So was Dana, but his mind was elsewhere. He tried to remember exactly what Benton had said that day.

I'm sure Benton never told me to say anything about the wedding his folks were going to, he thought over and over again.

Or did he?

6 • • •

Mrs. Bellamy looked across the table.

"Dana, did you lick your plate while I wasn't looking?" she asked.

"No, Mom, I got it all on my spoon," he replied. "Every last bite."

"Hmmmm, something must be on your mind," she said. "You always eat like an elephant when something's bothering you."

"No," he said. "I'm okay." Why upset her until he figured things out?

"Then you must be stashing it away for your father," she said, smiling. "You went through your dinner like . . . like a vacuum cleaner. Are you sure you don't have some strawberry shortcake up your sleeve?"

"Yuck!" said Christy. "That's messy. I'd only hide cookies up my sleeves."

Dana and Mrs. Bellamy laughed.

"No cookies for you — in fact nothing else for anyone tonight," Mrs. Bellamy said. "We don't want to become a bunch of fatties — especially with your father looking so thin."

Later that evening, Dana settled down in the big overstuffed chair in the living room to try to piece together the conversation he had had with Benton the day of the fire. He thought about those TV detective shows. When Perry Mason asked the questions, he expected a witness to remember every single word that was said, even if it happened years ago.

It wasn't that far back when the fire happened.

He remembered that he'd been walking home after practice when Benton told him about the wedding.

Did I ask if my folks should know about it? he thought. No, I'm sure I didn't. But I'm pretty sure he didn't ask me to tell my folks about it, either. But he thinks he did. Maybe I just don't remember it right.

Then a new thought struck him. He got up and walked around to think it through. Then he sat back down. Then he got up and walked around some more.

Could Benton know he didn't ask me to tell my folks — and be trying to cover up something? If so, then it's my word against his. Unless —

"Dana, what's wrong with you?" Christy's question interrupted his pondering. "You keep walking in front of the TV. Can't you see we're watching something?"

He hadn't even noticed his mother and sister come in and turn on the TV.

"Sorry," he mumbled. He stepped out of the way, trying to remember what he'd been thinking about. But Christy was yelling at the TV, and he couldn't concentrate.

"Our next contestant will give the wheel a spin," boomed a voice from the television set.

"Oooh, try a *B*, Steve, try a *B*!" Christy shouted.

Dana suddenly looked up. "That's it!" he cried.

"Calm down, Christy," said Mrs. Bellamy. "And you, too, Dana. The two of you are all wired up tonight. What's going on?"

"I'm just glad Dad's better," said Christy. "And he's going to come home soon. Yippee!"

"What about you, Dana? You're acting like a caged tiger."

"I've got to call Steve," Dana said, hurrying off to the kitchen.

His mother followed him.

"Dana, don't you think it's a little late in the evening to call Steve? What is it that can't wait until morning?"

Dana hesitated. He knew his mother shared Christy's happiness about their dad's improvement. How could he spoil her day by telling her about his problems with Benton? Besides, what could she do about it? He had to square things with Benton himself.

"I'm just glad Dad's getting better," he said.

Mrs. Bellamy pulled him over. She wrapped her arms around him and rubbed her chin on top of his head. "I'll tell you a little secret," she said. "The doctor told me there's no reason why Dad couldn't be home and back to work in just a few weeks. Isn't that great?"

"Terrific!" he said, and meant it. "You know

what? My call to Steve can wait. I think I'll hit the hay early tonight. See you in the morning."

"Ask for a vowel!" came the sound of Christy's voice in the living room.

Dana felt Mrs. Bellamy watch him head up to his room. He knew she wasn't convinced he had told her everything that was on his mind.

But suddenly Dana felt even more relieved about his father than he had realized. He got into bed, thinking that he'd talk to Steve first thing in the morning.

In less than a minute, he was sound asleep.

The next day was a Saturday.

"You lose, sleepyhead. I got the last of the good cereal," said Christy. She stirred her bowl of Sugar-O's around and around.

Dana smiled at her through a mouthful of corn-flakes. He felt too good this morning to care about unimportant things like that.

As soon as I finish up breakfast, he thought, I'll give Steve a call and get this whole mess with Benton cleared up once and for all.

The ringing of the telephone interrupted his thoughts.

"For you, Dana," Christy said. She handed him the cordless telephone.

Dana wiped his mouth. "Hello?" he said.

"Hey, Dana," came the reply. It was Steve. "What are you up to? Got some time to practice some kick shots?"

"I can't believe it. I was just thinking about you, Steve," said Dana. "Hang on a sec." He turned to his mother and asked, "Do you have any errands, Mom?"

"No."

"What about the hospital? When are we going to see Dad?"

"After lunch," she said.

"Meet you at the field?" he asked Steve.

"See you there."

"How soon?"

"Ten minutes?"

"Bet you ten extra kicks I get there before you," said Dana.

"Deal!"

Dana got dressed in a flash. He grabbed his soccer ball from the front hall closet and was off and running.

Still, as he rounded the corner to the field, he saw Steve. The Anchors' captain was dribbling around the goalpost making believe it was a defenseman.

"Okay, you win," Dana said. He tossed his ball toward Steve. "You can have five now and five later. But first I want to ask you something."

"Okay," said Steve.

"Remember the day Benton's house burned down?"

"Uh-huh."

"That was the day you were elected captain, right?"

"Right," Steve agreed.

"And we talked about it on the way home," Dana continued.

"After practice," said Steve.

"Do you remember Benton saying something about his folks going out that night?"

"Sure, they were going to a wedding. That's

where they were when the house caught on fire," said Steve.

"I know," said Dana. "But did Benton ask me to do anything?"

"Like what?" asked Steve. "He just said his parents were going to the wedding — that's all."

"He didn't ask me to tell my folks about it?"

"No," said Steve. "And I remember, too, 'cause I didn't know that they let him look after his kid sister when they went out. My folks still don't even like to leave me alone."

"Mine, too," said Dana. "They ask the Crawfords to keep an eye on us. And my folks do the same, when they're asked. I guess they just forgot to ask that time."

"Hey, are we here to practice, or what?" asked Steve.

He got into position while Dana ran over to the goal area.

They practiced for about a half hour. Then Steve suggested they take a break. The morning sun had been beating down on them, and they had worked up a good sweat.

They flopped down on the grass under a nearby maple tree.

"You have to remember to plant your left foot," said Steve. "You're rushing it and not getting into position."

"I'm just glad to have a load off my mind," said Dana.

"What? About Benton?"

Dana nodded. He told Steve about what Benton had said after the Cottoneers game.

"No way," said Steve. "I know what I heard. Hey, that must have been why he wasn't clicking with you during the game!"

"Wasn't clicking? Hey, it was like I was invisible!"

"Dana Bellamy, the great invisible right wing for the Anchors!" Steve laughed and threw the ball at Dana.

"Hey, guys!"

The high-pitched voice came from the side of the field.

Dana and Steve turned in that direction and saw a redheaded girl on a ten-speed bike. In the handlebar basket was a familiar video camera.

"Hey, Andrea," said Dana. "What are you doing here? Want to kick a few?"

She laughed. "Hardly!"

"She's probably going to make a movie about us," Steve suggested. "The town's own roving reporter is out to capture the two Anchors' rivals for top scorer as they secretly plot to share the crown!"

"I don't think this is going to make the six o'clock news," said Andrea. She flopped down on the grass next to them. "So you two guys are fighting it out for top scorer, huh?"

Dana knew Steve didn't really care who scored the most goals — as long as the team won.

"Nah, Steve's the best," said Dana.

"Dana's the natural," Steve insisted. "My job is to see to it that he gets a clear shot at the goal whenever possible."

"That's why he's the captain," said Dana.

"Yeah, I heard you were elected," said Andrea. "Unanimous decision, right?"

"Well, everyone voted for him in the end," said Dana. "I don't think Abe Strom was all that happy about it."

"Oh, I don't think he cared that much," said Steve.

"Oh, yeah?" said Dana. "I didn't see him passing the ball and setting you up much."

"Can't tell about these things, guys," Andrea said. "Maybe he still has a little chip on his shoulder."

"Think so?" Steve asked.

"Could be," said Dana. "Just like Benton."

"What about Benton?" Andrea asked.

Dana told her what happened in the Cottoneers game and afterward.

"Sounds to me like you guys have a lot of work to do," she said. "Not just practicing. You'd better get those guys to act like they're on a team or the Anchors are never going to win a game."

7 • • •

Dana had decided to clear the air with Benton before the next game. But his onetime pal and neighbor avoided him as if he had the plague. Even in homeroom, Benton kept away from him. Whenever Dana tried to speak with him, Benton either ran off or got into a conversation with another kid.

It was the same during practice. Benton only passed the ball to him when absolutely necessary. Dana knew he had to get that chip off of Benton's shoulder — and soon, or else the team as well as their friendship would be in trouble.

But he just couldn't corner Benton between classes, and he was nowhere to be found during lunch. By the time the game with the Grizzlies rolled around, Dana was finding it hard to believe that he and Benton had ever been friends at all.

The game with the Grizzlies was scheduled for four o'clock. Dana got there early and made sure Steve was nearby to back him up just in case Benton continued to accuse him of forgetfulness.

But Benton didn't show up until just before the game began.

"Move it, Crawford," called Coach Kingsley. "I was almost ready to put someone else into your slot."

The Anchors and the Grizzlies settled into their positions, and the game began.

The brown-and-green uniformed Grizzlies were in third place in the league, only a few games behind the leader. But their standing didn't tell the whole story. They had lost most of their games by only one goal. There was no doubt they were a dangerous opponent.

Less than five minutes had gone by when the first goal was scored — by the Grizzlies. Their star right wing, Buzz Saw Wallace, had drilled a kick past Jazz's outstretched arms.

The first mark went up on the scoreboard: Grizzlies 1, Anchors 0.

"Come on, you guys! Let's wake up!" Steve yelled.

The two teams positioned themselves at opposite sides of the center line. Dana took a good look at Buzz Saw. He deserved his nickname. He was short and chunky, but he could cut through the defense like a power-driven blade.

When the starting whistle blew, Steve tapped the ball to Dana. Dana booted it to Jack Nguyen, who stopped it with his hip and took control. He dribbled toward the Grizzlies' goal. As he worked his way down the field, the Grizzlies' defense closed in on him. Waiting for him at the goal line, the Grizzlies' goalie, Noonie Mills, crouched like a big brown bear guarding his cave.

Dana ran toward Jack from the right. Slightly behind him he could see Benton coming up the field. Suddenly a Grizzlies tackler swooped down on Jack and tried to get the ball. But Jack managed to shake loose enough to pass it to Benton.

Benton trapped it with his right foot and

dribbled it steadily toward the goal. Dana was surprised to hear him hacking and coughing as he gained ground. It sounded like he had a miserable cold.

Before Benton could get in position to try a goal kick, he was surrounded. A bunch of Grizzlies ganged up on him from his rear and his left.

On his right side, Dana was in the clear.

"Bent! Over here!" Dana called softly — just loud enough for Benton to hear.

Benton glanced at him briefly. For a second, it seemed as though he would pass the ball to the open wing.

But he didn't. Instead, he wriggled free enough to boot the ball toward the goal. He was in no position to make it good. There wasn't even much of a chance that the ball would make it all the way to the goal area.

Benton should have seen that, Dana thought. He just doesn't want me to have a shot. The anger rose up in him like lava in a volcano.

Noonie Mills caught the ball easily and tossed it over to a Grizzlies fullback. The action now moved down toward the Anchors' goal.

Reversing direction, Dana ran after Benton.

"You bug me, you know that?" Dana shouted at him. "You have it in for me for no good reason!"

"You messed up! You should have —," Benton began. Before he could finish, a coughing spell cut him off.

"You're a real blockhead, Benton!" Dana shouted back. "You don't even know what you're talking about!"

"Knock it off!" Steve's loud voice boomed. "Knock it off, or I'll ask the coach to bench the two of you!"

Dana saw the stern look on Steve's face. He knew he meant every word of it. Friend or not, the Anchor captain didn't make idle threats, not when the game was at stake.

Dana tried to put his mind back on the game. He had his eye on a fight for the ball between Lance and a Grizzlies tackler when Abe sidled up next to him.

"What are you yelling about? Someone else got a shot for a change?" he said, sneering at Dana.

Then he ran off to his own side of the field.

Dana was shocked.

What was going on? Had Benton told everyone on the team that he was responsible for the fire? Was the whole team on his case?

What was that going to do to their chance of winning this game — or any game, for that matter?

Even if only some of the guys got all hung up, they'd mess up the whole team. The Grizzlies could score a dozen goals they didn't deserve, just because the Anchors were all bent out of shape.

He had to straighten Benton out. But first there was a game to play.

Down at the other end of the field, Mike, Tucker, and Pete were fighting for the ball with two Grizzlies forwards. From between their legs, the ball squirted out and bounced onto the open field.

Jonathan Bell, the Grizzlies' right halfback, sprinted after it. He gave it a kick that sent it rocketing toward the right side of the goal.

Jazz made a flying leap for it. He was within inches when the ball sizzled by and into the net for another Grizzlies score.

Dana's heart sank. Midway through the first half and the Anchors were in deep trouble.

Things didn't change much during the remainder of the half. The two teams seemed to shuffle back and forth, with both defenses digging in. There was a lot of motion, a few penalties, and a couple of goal attempts. But there was no scoring. When the half ended, the scoreboard still read Grizzlies 2, Anchors 0.

During the halftime break, Coach Kingsley tried to pump some spirit into the Anchors.

"What's with you guys today?" he asked. "I know you're capable of much more! You look like you're playing with blinders on!"

There was a lot of foot scuffling. Most of the players stared down at their cleats.

"Some of you haven't noticed that that's a soccer field you're playing on, not a bowling alley. You're not out there on your own. So start looking around and pass the ball. Got that?"

"Right, Coach!"

"Got it!"

No one could disagree. They just weren't playing like a team.

The coach gazed around, then settled his eyes on some of the players near the back of the huddle.

After a few awkward moments, he cleared his throat and laid out a plan of attack.

"Now, listen, and listen good," the coach said firmly. "We've had a half dozen chances of shooting for a goal, but you blew it every time. I know there isn't time to set up a lot of fancy plays, but you have to have some discipline. Remember, when you're bringing the ball downfield, stay in your positions and try to get the ball to one of the wings. One or the other, not always the same one. And wings, you find a way to get yourself into position to kick. Keep the ball moving — just keep it moving. Everybody got the picture?"

"Got it!" they all shouted again.

"Okay, then — get out there and show me some teamwork!"

Dana didn't know whether the coach was getting through to Benton, or to Abe, or to anyone else. He would just have to wait and see.

It wasn't long before he got an answer.

As soon as the Anchors got the ball, Tucker, Lance, and Abe kept it over on the left side of the field. Now and then, Jack or Steve got a pass booted their way, but Dana might as well have been sitting in the stands.

Buzz Saw, however, was all over the place. He stole the ball from Abe and broke away clear down to the goal. There was no way Jazz could hold him off alone. All by himself, Buzz Saw booted one in for the Grizzlies' third goal of the game.

The scoreboard now read Grizzlies 3, Anchors 0.

"Defense! Defense!" shouted the Anchors' fans in the stands.

But the offense is just as bad, Dana thought angrily. They're working as hard at keeping the ball away from *me* as they are at trying to score.

As the second half progressed, the ball occasionally found its way to Dana — mostly on mix-ups and wild scrambles.

Whenever he did get the ball, though, he didn't hold on to it long. "Keep it moving," the coach had said — and he did. Besides, if the team saw that he was doing his best, maybe they would wake up.

They didn't. About ten minutes into the second

half, Lance had the ball. Dana was all by himself with no one between him and the goal. It would have been an easy pass and a sure shot at a goal. But Lance booted it over to Abe. And as usual, a pack of Grizzlies was all over the Anchors' left wing in seconds.

Meanwhile, Benton strayed out of his zone and recovered a rebound off a stray Grizzlies backfielder.

"Go for it, Benton!" Dana shouted. Even if he wasn't getting any shots at the goal, at least someone might put them on the scoreboard.

But Benton started moving so fast, he tripped over the ball and collapsed in a heap.

The loose ball ended up in front of Steve. He dribbled it toward the goal, then passed it to Dana, who was nearby on his right.

Dana trapped the ball, dribbled it a few feet, then pulled his right foot back. He got under the ball with his laces and booted it toward the left side of the goal. It was an angle shot and tough by any count. But the Grizzlies' goalie was way out of range. He couldn't get anywhere near it in time.

The black-and-white leather sphere rammed into the net for a goal.

Dana's heart swelled as he heard the crowd roar. Then the Anchors' cheerleaders took up the cry:

> *Give me a D!*
> *D!*
> *Give me an A!*
> *A!*
> *Give me an N!*
> *N!*
> *Give me an A!*
> *A!*
> *What do you have?*
> *Dana! Dana! Dana!*
> *Hooray!*

8 • • •

Steve came running over and gave Dana a high five. But with a 3–1 score and the clock ticking away, there was no time to waste. If the Anchors were going to make any headway, they had to get the ball back quickly.

Abe took care of that. After the starting kick, he bore down on Buzz Saw Wallace and took the ball away with some fancy footwork. Then he booted it downfield all the way to Steve, who was in the clear.

Steve brought it into the penalty area before he was sandwiched between two Grizzlies tacklers. He got off a little flick pass to Benton before they completely boxed him in.

Wheezing and puffing, Benton took the ball almost into the goal area before he, too, was surrounded.

He could have passed it to me, Dana said to himself, sighing. He could have.

Instead, Benton heel-kicked the ball. Jack went for it, but it got by him. The Grizzlies took control and broke away toward the goal.

Thunk!

The ball went crashing into the net for another score.

Grizzlies 4, Anchors 1.

"We still can do it!" shouted Steve. "Come on, you Anchors!"

Steve hasn't given up, and neither will I, Dana said to himself as play continued.

But it would take more than their determination, he knew. The rest of the team had to pitch in.

A few seconds later, Dana got another chance to help out the Anchors with a score. A midfield snarl had produced a drop ball. Jack was on the spot for the Anchors.

The ball squiggled over to Lance, who passed it on to Steve. The Anchors' captain dribbled the ball toward the goal as best he could. A swarm of Grizzlies bore down on him from all sides.

Steve glanced to his left, then to his right. Then he kicked the ball with the instep of his left foot in Dana's direction.

Running after it with all the speed he could muster, Dana got to the ball a split second before a hungry Grizzlies defenseman.

Over on the far side of the field, Lance and Abe made a big show of calling for the pass from Dana. But the Anchors' right wing booted the ball swiftly back to Steve.

Steve trapped it with his left foot. For a moment, it looked like he would go for a goal kick even though the path was blocked. He drew back his foot — then surprised everyone by flicking the ball over to Dana.

All alone and in the clear, Dana trapped the ball. He then quickly sent it flying toward the goal.

It was a perfect shot.

Goal!

The score now read: Grizzlies 4, Anchors 2.

"All right!" Dana shouted, waving his fist in the

air. See, guys, the coach was right, he wanted to add. Teamwork pays off.

"Nice work, Dana!" Steve called over to him.

"Thanks, Steve," he replied. "Thanks for the pass."

As play started up again, Dana caught Benton's eye. There was no joy beaming in his direction from that corner of the field.

There was no time to worry about Benton and his deep freeze act now. He would take care of that later.

The Anchors seemed to be coming alive. That's what mattered. Now if they could only hold off the Grizzlies — and keep that ball moving among themselves. It was their only hope. But everyone had to do his part. Everyone had to play one hundred percent for the team.

As he ran upfield to get in position for a pass from the defense, Dana could see Benton lagging behind. At one point, he saw him lean over, hands on knees, panting for breath.

No one else seemed to notice.

"Benton, are you okay?" he called.

But Benton straightened up, shot him a look, and rejoined the action.

Two Grizzlies were passing the ball back and forth in the Anchors' penalty area. Jack was ping-ponging back and forth between them when Pete worked his way in and stole the ball.

Jack broke loose and trapped Pete's pass. He booted the ball back downfield, toward the Grizzlies' goal. It almost went out of bounds near the midfield stripe when Benton stopped it.

He twisted around to start moving it toward the goal. But two Grizzlies were in his way, so instead, he booted it over to Abe. Then he rushed off toward the goal.

Before Benton could get there, a coughing fit overtook him. Again, he doubled over hacking and wheezing.

Abe searched frantically for someone in the clear.

There was no one in front of him, but Dana was only ten feet to his right, all by himself.

"Abe!" Dana shouted. "Over here!" Frantically, he waved and shouted.

Abe ignored him. Instead, he tried to dribble the ball forward. He managed to squeeze by a few

Grizzlies tacklers and gain a few more yards. He glanced in Dana's direction, then toward the goal. Then, seconds before a Grizzlies fullback reached him, Abe gave the ball a hard, solid boot. It went zooming toward the goal.

But it never made it. The Grizzlies defender blocked the ball right in front of the goal line.

"Abe!" Dana yelled. "I was clear! Why didn't you pass the ball?"

"Didn't see you," Abe muttered.

Dana stared at him. It's like he's taking Benton's side, he thought angrily. I can't believe Abe would turn against me just because he thinks I didn't tell my parents about a wedding! But what else could it be?

For a moment, Dana felt like quitting. What good was it to keep on playing all by himself? How could he pretend there was an Anchors team on the field?

On the other hand, what would quitting accomplish? It might even make the guys think Benton was right, that he had somehow been responsible for the fire. No, he had to keep on playing.

Some fancy footwork by the Grizzlies put the

ball back in Anchors territory, where they struggled to defend their goal. Dana stayed out of the thick of things, hoping the ball would come his way rather than Jazz's.

Then he finally got it, on a forward pass from Jack. He started dribbling down the field, looking for an open receiver.

But it seemed he was all alone. Steve was closely covered, and Benton seemed hardly able to keep up, he was wheezing so hard. Luckily, through some really good moves and fancy dribbling, Dana held off the enemy.

Look at this, you wise guys, he thought, who needs all of you?

Then, while his head was all swelled up, a Grizzlies tackler snatched the ball right out from under his nose.

Dana stood there in a daze.

"Should've passed it, dummy!" a voice behind him shouted.

It was Lance. The Anchor halfback gave him a look that could have turned a green banana to brown. Then he dashed back into Anchors territory, where the Grizzlies were again threatening.

Dana broke out of his fog and raced down the field along with the rest of the team.

He couldn't get over it. *Dummy!* Lance never called anybody names.

Coach Kingsley must have heard the comment. He signaled for Lance to come out. Mac Reese went in for him.

But Mac only got to play for a few minutes before the whistle blew.

The game ended with a victory for the Grizzlies, 4–2.

Dana knew he couldn't let the rotten situation go on. He had to clear things up with Benton.

The coach was obviously disappointed in the way the Anchors had played. Before they left the field, he called them over to one side.

"I think you all know what's going wrong," he said. "I'm not going to say anything more until next practice. Everyone had better be there!"

Benton turned to pick up his knapsack. As he lifted it off the bench, a T-shirt covered with dark smudges fell out.

Dana stooped down and picked it up. He thought the shirt smelled like smoke, but before he could be sure, Benton had whisked it out of his hands and stuffed it back into his sack.

Dana planted himself in front of his teammate. Angry as he was, he could hear his mom's voice saying, "You can catch more flies with honey than with vinegar." Okay, he decided, I'll give it a try.

As gently as possible, he asked, "Benton, I've been wanting to talk to you all week. I tried to get you before the game today, but you weren't here. I think we need to clear the air about — "

Benton suddenly straightened up and snapped at him. "I don't have anything to say to you — or anyone else in your family!"

"Wait a minute!" Dana protested. "You can't keep blaming me or my folks for what happened to your house. You never asked me to tell my mom and dad that your folks were going out that night. It wasn't their fault the fire got out of control!"

"Oh, yeah?" Benton sneered. "Well, for your information, the fire was all your father's fault in the first place!"

Dana was dumbfounded. "My father? You're nuts!"

"You think so? Your old man, the 'brilliant' electrician, did a lousy wiring job on our house. If it

wasn't for that, we'd still be living there, not across town in some crummy apartment. And . . . and I wouldn't be coughing so much from the smoke that got in my lungs from the fire!"

"Benton! How can you say that? The smoke must have gotten into your brain!"

"My mother told me. She said it all happened on account of electrical problems. And your father rewired our house last year, so it's all his fault!"

Dana stared at him in disbelief.

"She's wrong! My dad's an electrical engineer. He designs wiring for new houses and stores and offices. There's no one who knows more about electricity and wiring, and . . . and the fire couldn't have happened 'cause of his work!"

By now, just about everyone had left the field. Some of the Anchors and fans were down near the entrance gate. Benton had gotten his wind back and rushed off to join them.

"Besides," Dana called after him, "you're forgetting one big thing. My dad saved your life! And your sister's! And — "

But by this time, Benton was beyond the sound of his voice.

9 • • •

"Four to two, that's a shame," said Mrs. Bellamy. "But Dana, you scored both goals for your team. You must be very proud — and happy, at least, about that."

"Uh-huh," Dana replied. He closed the car door and slumped down in the seat.

"You don't sound all that cheerful," she said.

"Are you and Benton mad at each other?" Christy piped up from the backseat. "I saw you looking at him like he was poison — and he acted like you were the 'lectric chair."

Dana hesitated. He just couldn't keep it to himself. Benton's accusation was too . . . too . . . it was rotten!

"Benton's a no-good, miserable, dirty —"

"Whoa! Wait a minute!" exclaimed Mrs. Bellamy.

"What's going on? You don't use that kind of language, Dana."

"Well, Benton said something really bad."

"Did he use a naughty word, like — "

"Christy!" Mrs. Bellamy snapped. "Quiet down! Now, Dana, what did Benton say?"

Dana gritted his teeth. "He said his mother told him it was Dad's fault their house caught on fire."

"What?" Mrs. Bellamy's hands clutched the steering wheel. "Grace Crawford blames the fire on your father?"

"Uh-huh. She says the house caught on fire because of an electrical problem. And 'cause Dad did the rewiring, the Crawfords blame him."

"This is incredible," said Mrs. Bellamy. "How could the Crawfords jump to such a hasty conclusion?"

"Why would Dad want to burn down their house, anyhow?" Christy said, fuming. "It's stupid. The Crawfords are stupid!"

"Christy, behave yourself," said Mrs. Bellamy. "I'm sure the fire upset Grace very badly. So naturally, she's grasping at anything she thinks might be an answer to why it happened. And when she heard *electrical*, well, one thing led to another."

"Sounds pretty weak to me," said Dana.

"As far as I know, the insurance company hasn't finished its investigation," Mrs. Bellamy went on. "No one can be sure how the fire started."

"I'm just telling you what Benton said," Dana insisted. Then something occcurred to him. "Maybe he told the guys on the team! That could be why Abe and Lance are ganging up on me."

"I'll give Grace a call," said Mrs. Bellamy. "Meanwhile, let's not make things worse by jumping to any conclusions like that, Dana. And don't say anything about this to your father. We don't want to worry him while he's getting better. He'd have a fit!"

When they arrived at Mr. Bellamy's room, they found him sitting up. He was sipping ginger ale through a bent straw. Both of his hands were free. There wasn't a single tube sticking into him.

"Way to go, Dad," said Dana cheerfully. "You ought to be leaving here pretty soon, right?"

"Not as soon as I'd like," said Mr. Bellamy. "Doc Higgins said they have to monitor my breathing for a few more days. They want to make sure there are no glitches . . . or whatever he called it."

"Last thing you want is a case of glitches," said Mrs. Bellamy, smiling at him.

"Right, Dad," said Christy. "They're almost as bad as the itches."

"Or even worse, the twitches," suggested Dana.

"Or the snitches," said Christy.

"The britches," offered Dana.

"The kritches!" shouted Christy.

Mr. Bellamy pinched his nose and grunted, "*Braaaaack!* No such word. You lose. By the way, how did your game go, Dana?"

"*Lose* is the right word," Dana admitted. "We lost, four to two. But, well, I scored both goals."

"Both goals? Wow, you must be right up there with Steve Rapids."

"Yeah, I guess we're tied now," said Dana. "Funny, I haven't even thought about that."

"Good," said Mr. Bellamy. "It's more important to concentrate on teamwork. I'm still proud of you. Come on over here," he beckoned.

Mr. Bellamy raised one arm and slowly extended his open palm.

Dana caught the signal. He went over to the bed and gave his father a gentle high five.

Mrs. Phillips marched into the room waving a thermometer. "I think that's enough excitement in this room for today," she declared. "Besides, it's almost time for our snack."

"Hot fudge sundae with marshmallow and chopped walnuts?" asked Mr. Bellamy with a twinkle in his eye.

"Cranberry juice and a vanilla cookie," she said.

Mr. Bellamy groaned.

As Dana, his mom, and Christy piled into the car in the hospital parking lot a few minutes later, Dana said, "If Dad knew what the Crawfords are saying, he would —"

"Let me worry about that," said Mrs. Bellamy. "I'll talk to Grace Crawford and see if we can clear that up."

Dana strapped on his seat belt. He wasn't sure that would be enough. He had to find a way to clear his father's name and shut Benton up once and for all.

*   *   *

It was barely daylight when Dana got out of bed the next morning. He dressed quietly, then tip-toed downstairs. As he opened the hall closet to get his jacket, he noticed that the kitchen light was on.

The closet door squeaked as he pushed it shut.

"Dana? Christy? Who's up so early?" came a voice from the kitchen.

Dana found his mother seated at the round oak kitchen table. She held a steaming cup of coffee in her hand.

"Aren't you the early bird!" she said.

"I . . . uh . . . just wanted to get outside and . . . uh . . . have a look around," he mumbled. "Did you call Mrs. Crawford?"

"I called last night. Got an answering machine," Mrs. Bellamy said. "I left a message, but I haven't heard from her yet."

"Figures," said Dana.

"That's not nice, Dana," she said. "And what do you mean 'have a look around'?"

"Mmmmmm, you know. See what I can find out."

"Dana, I don't want you going near the Crawford house. It's dangerous. Just keep away. The insurance company will find out how the fire started. That will clear everything up."

"But —," Dana started to protest.

"No *buts* about it," she said firmly. "Now, just put away your jacket and come sit down. I'll make your favorite breakfast — buttermilk pancakes."

He knew she wouldn't change her mind, so he did as she said. But he was sure the pancakes would stick in his throat.

The situation at school was pretty much the same as on the field. Benton avoided him. Abe and Lance weren't as obvious, but he could still feel a chill around them.

Never mind, he thought, I have other things on my mind — like this geography test staring me in the face.

There were a lot of blank spaces on his paper when the bell rang at the end of class.

When he turned in the test, Ms. Thompson, the geography teacher, looked it over quickly.

"Dana Bellamy!" she called just before he got out the door.

She looked him straight in the eye. "You haven't answered even half the questions. Your work has gone downhill in the last few days. Is there something wrong?"

How could he tell her what was bothering him? Was he going to say, "Benton's mad at me," like a two-year-old? Or "Benton's telling lies about my father," like a four-year-old? No, he had to handle this on his own.

"I've had a lot on my mind" was all he could admit.

Ms. Thompson sighed. "Yes, I know about your father being in the hospital. But it's not going to help him to hear that you're failing in school, Dana. How is he progressing, by the way?"

"He's a lot better," said Dana. "We expect him home any time now."

"Good," said Ms. Thompson. "Then we can expect your work to start improving. We'll give it a few days and then talk about a makeup test."

"Thanks a lot, Ms. Thompson," said Dana, making his exit.

Instead of eating lunch in the school cafeteria, he took his sandwich and carton of milk outside. He settled down in a quiet spot, mostly surrounded by trees and bushes, to study for his afternoon classes. He had to do better on his schoolwork.

Staring off into space, he tried to memorize some dates for history class. His eyes drifted to a corner of the school yard near the equipment shed. About half a dozen kids were hanging out there, trying to shelter one another.

They were smoking. This was strictly against school policy, but some kids did it anyway. If anyone came near them, they threw the evidence into the nearby Dumpster.

Dana caught a distant shout that sounded like "Hey, Bent!"

He gazed across the field and saw Benton ambling toward the shed.

When he got within twenty yards of the shed, Benton glanced back at the school building. For a split second, Dana thought Benton was looking right at him. But Benton turned away sharply and reversed direction. Putting on some speed, he jogged over to the side entrance of the school and disappeared.

What was that all about? Dana wondered. Then the bell rang and, with a sigh, he closed his notebook and headed into the building.

At the end of soccer practice that afternoon, Coach Kingsley had the team sit down in one long row on the bench. Then he walked up and down in front of them. He told them he was unhappy about the way they had been playing their games.

"If you have problems off the field, leave them there," he said. "This is a game of teamwork. You have to be looking around all the time to help out the rest of the team. And the rest of the team has to help you out. That goes for each and every one of you: wings, backs, goalie — the whole lot.

"Now, we have a game with the Rams coming up on Thursday. When you show up for the game, show up to play on a *team*. If you can't do that, don't show up!"

Dana caught the coach looking at him and Benton with more than the usual eye contact. Coach knows there's something going on, he said to himself. Does he know what Benton's been saying? Does he think the fire's my fault — or my dad's?

But there was no sign that Coach Kingsley had anything on his mind except getting the Anchors to play winning soccer.

10 • • •

The game with the Norristown Rams was about to start.

Coach Kingsley gave the Anchors a few final words of advice.

"We bungled our last two games," he reminded them, "because we forgot we're a team. Let's not bungle this one! Forwards, set yourselves up to score. Halfbacks, set up the forwards. Fullbacks, you have to be the solid wall of defense.

"You're not going to win this game with a lot of fancy plays. But you have to keep your eyes open and take advantage of your opportunities. Move the ball around and play as a team!"

"Team! Team! Anchors!" they all shouted, slapping high fives and tens all around.

The coin was flipped. This time, Steve made the call.

"Tails!" he shouted.

Tails it was. The Anchors chose to kick. The Rams elected to defend the north goal.

At the whistle, Steve kicked the ball to Jack. Jack aimed a kick right back at him, but booted it too hard. It landed midway into Rams territory before it touched down. Play was underway.

Louie Ladd, the Rams' center halfback, took it almost to the midfield stripe. Lance moved in on him and blocked him from gaining any more ground.

They struggled for the ball before it squirted loose to the left side of the field. Abe was in position and snagged it. He started to move it toward the goal, then quickly passed it to Steve.

The Anchors' captain didn't have an open shot at the goal, so he passed it over to Benton.

Benton moved the ball a few feet before a Rams tackler blocked his way.

Dana saw the tackler starting to breathe down on Benton. He broke away from his own blocker and worked his way over in Benton's direction. He wondered whether Benton would give him the ball.

He soon found out.

Benton held out until he saw an opening behind him. He twisted around and just got off a little flick pass to Jack.

But Jack wasn't really in the clear. He had to struggle with a Ram tackler for the ball. The two of them were tangling legs when suddenly the whistle blew.

Tweeeet!

The referee turned toward Jack. The call was "Holding!"

From where Dana stood, there was no doubt about it. Jack had grabbed the Ram's arm and tried to shove him away.

The ref placed the ball on the ground where the penalty was called. The Anchors and the Rams backed away the regulation ten yards.

The Ram's kick was bad. The ball slanted toward Steve. He caught it between his ankles, then started moving it toward the goal again.

As the rest of the Anchors' offense started running in that direction, Dana caught Benton's eye. The right halfback just shrugged, with an innocent look on his face. Dana shook his head. Some people never learn, he thought. The coach might as well have talked to a wall.

By now the play had shifted back to Anchors territory. The Rams had taken the ball away before the Anchors could even get close to the goal.

Louie Ladd was threatening. He took a pass from the Rams' left wing and turned toward the goal. There was no one near him. He drew back, ran forward, planted his left foot, and kicked with his right.

The kick was a beauty — about four feet off the ground and angled straight toward the goal.

But once again, Jazz came through. He trapped the kick with his chest and picked up the ball in the goal area. Then he booted it solidly downfield. The long, high kick took the ball some ten yards from the center line, just to the edge of the circle.

Players from both teams raced after it. Dana halfheartedly approached the crowd scrambling for the loose ball.

Jack Nguyen shook it loose. His toe got under

the ball as he passed it over to Steve. The ball rose in the air, and Steve stopped it with his head.

Luckily he was facing the right direction. The ball went careening into Rams territory.

Dana bolted after it, trapped the ball, then dribbled it a couple of yards.

Heads up, he thought. He looked around. There was Benton, running parallel with him on his left side. He was looking for the pass.

For one moment, Dana wanted to treat Benton the same way everyone had treated *him*. You've ignored me, he thought — now I can do the same to you. But in the blink of an eye, he realized he'd be acting as dumb as everyone else. He'd be no better than Benton — and he'd be letting the coach and the team down. We have to play as a team, no matter what, he said to himself.

He flicked the ball over to Benton, who trapped it with the inside of his left foot. Without looking at Dana, he started moving it downfield, toward the goal.

Was he surprised that I passed it to him? Dana wondered. Who knows?

Two Ram tacklers now converged on Benton. He aimed a kick toward a cluster of Anchors down near the goal, but the ball never made it that far. It ricocheted off the leg of one of his tacklers and bounced back upfield.

Once again, the play shifted direction. As he ran upfield, Dana was surprised to hear Benton hacking and coughing up ahead of him. Is he still suffering from smoke he breathed in during the fire? Dana wondered. Maybe it did some serious damage to his lungs, after all. But Dad inhaled a lot more smoke. Look how much better he is now. . . .

He couldn't think about that any longer. The ball was loose in his general area of the field, just beyond the midfield line in Rams territory.

Dana got to it in time to trap it with the inside of his right foot. He kept it under control until he saw an opening. Here was his chance to set up a goal.

Eye on the ball, he booted a long pass downfield toward Lance. The Anchors' left halfback was all by himself. But he stumbled when the ball came to him. He just managed to trap the ball before the Rams' defense bore down on him.

Lance had to get rid of the ball. Dana, who had sped up along the right wing slot, was the only player in the clear. It was lose the ball or pass to him.

Before Lance had a chance to do either, one of the Rams tacklers stole the ball away. He dribbled it to one side of the field, then booted it toward the Anchors' goal.

But his own teammate got in the way. The ball bounced off the leg of the other tackler and over to Dana.

The rest of the Rams were moving toward Anchors territory. Dana had plenty of time to set up a good kick.

He sent the ball rocketing toward the Rams' goal.

For a moment, he thought the kick would be good. But their goalie caught it about a yard in front of the goal. He wasted no time sending it back downfield.

Dana recovered and turned in that direction. He found himself racing side by side with Benton.

They went after the ball, each one trying to get there first.

They both reached it pretty much at the same time.

"Get out of here!" Benton snapped. "I'll take it!"

Dana stared at him. Why should he give up the ball to Benton? Who said Benton could decide?

Benton struggled to control the ball. His breath was coming in gasps. The ball wiggled free, and Dana took it away.

By now a bunch of Rams was bearing down on the two of them. Dana tried to set up a breakaway. He booted the ball way down the field, in the direction of the Rams' goal. With any luck, Abe or Steve would get to it in time for a goal attempt.

Steve almost had it, but there were too many Rams crowding around him. He struggled for control, but finally lost the ball to a Rams tackler. The ball went back upfield as play shifted once again.

The Anchors' defense did their best to hold them. They might have succeeded if Tucker hadn't fallen. The Anchors' fullback had charged into a crowd of Rams trying to snag the ball. He almost had it when he slipped on the grass and fell on his butt.

The rest of the Anchors had held back, waiting to take over the ball from Tucker. Now there was no one in the way. The Rams' right wing took his shot. He sent the ball flying to the left side of the goal area, just beyond Jazz's reach. The ball went in for the game's first score.

The goal brought out the Rams' supporters in full force. Dana couldn't help but hear their cheers ring out.

> *Rams, yell 'Red'!*
> *Red!*
> *Rams, yell 'White'!*
> *White!*
> *Rams, yell 'Win'!*
> *Win!*
> *Rams, what do you say?*
> *Red! White! Win!*

A blur of red-and-white ribbons waved in the air.

The Anchors' cheerleaders weren't about to take

that sitting down. They rallied the crowd in their section of the stands.

> *Brickety-axe, co-axe, co-axe,*
> *Hullabaloo, baloo,*
> *Anchors fight with all your might,*
> *Hurrah, for the red and blue!*
> *Anchors, Anchors, rah, rah, rah!*

Dana smiled. Too bad the team on the field wasn't as feisty. Too bad they couldn't seem to get their act together. Too bad they weren't playing as a team.

11 • • •

There were only seven minutes left in the first half, with the Rams still leading, 1–0.

"How are you doing?" Steve asked.

Dana shrugged. "Okay."

"You sure?"

Dana shrugged again, but this time kept silent. They jogged side by side down the field.

"I had a little talk with Benton," Steve said.

"You did? About what?"

"I told him to knock off those stories about the fire and about your father."

"You heard what he said about my dad's work?" Dana almost stopped in his tracks.

"You bet I did," Steve said. "So I asked my dad about your father. He told me there isn't a better electrician anywhere. Your dad did some work for him on a real estate development last year and saved him a bundle. Plus the workmanship was terrific, he said."

Dana's heart swelled with pride.

"So when I told him about the rumor going around, he got real angry," Steve went on. "I figured it was time I put an end to it."

Dana's mouth was so dry, he could hardly speak. But he managed to get out, "Thanks, Steve. Thanks a lot!"

By then they were just inside the center line.

"Let's get that ball!" Steve shouted to his fellow Anchors.

Dana headed over to the far corner of the field. He felt stronger and better than he had in a long time.

But the Rams held on to the ball. The Anchors' defense bore down, but they couldn't stem the tide. Within a matter of seconds, the Rams had the ball inside the goal area.

Watching Pete and Tucker trying to wrench the ball from a Rams halfback, Dana stood with his fists clenched. His knees were bent, ready to go after the ball if it came his way. All the while, he shouted encouragement.

"Come on, Tuck! Come on, Pete! Get that ball!"

In the midst of all the noise from both sides, someone must have heard him. He couldn't tell who it was, but that someone sent the ball zooming straight at him.

He was after it in a shot. Steve led the rest of the offense in the same direction. But the ball was all Dana's. He trapped it with his chest, let it drop, then dribbled it toward midfield. Off to one side, he could see Jack Nguyen running parallel with him, waiting for a pass. At the same time, Rams tacklers were moving in, getting closer and closer. He could almost hear their breathing.

He got within striking range, but there was a wall of defenders between him and the goal. He swiveled to one side, then turned to the other and passed the ball to Jack.

Jack had the ball all by himself. There was one Ram fullback between him and a possible score.

"Make it a winner, Jack!" Dana yelled.

Jack drew back and booted the ball. But he had aimed his foot too high. Instead of flying through the air, the ball skittered on the grass.

Abe and Steve swooped down after it. Abe got to it first. He kicked at it, slicing it back toward Dana.

Dana trapped the ball with his feet. He dribbled it a few feet toward the goal, then positioned himself for the kick. He gave it his best shot.

The ball took off like a meteor.

Never had he kicked a ball that hard — and within microseconds, he wished he could pull it back. Abe had somehow gotten between Dana and the goal. The ball hit him in the back with a sickening thud. The force was so great, it knocked him over. The ball bounced over the goal line.

"Abe!" Dana cried as the whistle sounded. The ref helped Abe to his feet, then positioned the ball for a goal kick. The Rams' goalie booted it with all his might.

There was a lot of groaning among the Anchors. But Abe only gave Dana a silent, steely glare.

With a minute to go in the half, the Rams were

threatening again. In fact, it seemed like an instant replay of the action before their goal earlier in the game.

Again, Dana was a little outside the tangled struggle for the ball. As much as he wanted to get in there, he knew he had to stick to his position.

Just when he was sure a penalty whistle would blow, the ball broke loose. Sam Mikula, the Rams' left wing, snagged it. With only seconds left to play, he got set and booted the ball toward the goal. Jazz dived for it with all his might, but that wasn't enough. He was at least two feet from the ball when it zipped between the goalposts and struck the back of the net.

It sounded like the Fourth of July as the whistle finally signaled the end of the first half. The crowd erupted, and the Rams celebrated the score: 2–0, in their favor.

"Tough luck, Dana," Coach Kingsley said as the Anchors' wing came off the field. "We almost had one there. If your kick had just been a few more inches to one side, it would have been in there."

"That kick was hard enough to knock over an elephant," said Steve, settling down on the bench.

It sure had knocked over Abe, Dana thought. Now he and Benton have another reason to gripe about me.

The coach reviewed the first half with them. He pointed out problems, like not enough passing and lack of concentration.

"When you get the ball, look around," he told them. "Figure out where you want to go, what you want to do with it. Then act fast. Don't just grab the ball and plunge straight ahead into a mess in the middle."

He made a few final points. Then he called Dana and Benton over to one side.

"Look, I don't know what's going on between you two," he said quietly. "But whatever it is, cut it out. You're hurting the team. So don't take your personal problems out on the field with you.

"I'm surprised at the two of you. You're neighbors. And everyone knows that Dana's father saved your life, Benton. So, will someone please tell me what's the problem?"

"Nothing," said Benton, staring at the ground.

"Nothing? Hey, I'm not blind, Benton. I can see the freeze going on out there. What about you, Dana? Are you going to tell me it's nothing, too?"

Dana shuffled his toe in the grass. "All I know is that Benton's going around saying it's my family's fault his house burned down to the ground."

Benton started to say something, but choked out a cough instead.

"He says my dad did a lousy job wiring their house, too, and that's how the fire started. But he's wrong! My dad —"

"My mother ought to know. She says an electrical problem caused the fire!" Benton cut in bitterly.

"That doesn't mean anything," Dana argued. " 'Sides, she's just guessing!"

"What do you know, anyhow? You can't even remember when someone asks you to do something!" Benton snapped.

"Okay, you two, knock it off — right now!" said the coach. "Listen, if you both want to keep playing for this team, you put all that out of your minds and play ball. Sounds like you're both shooting your mouths off too much. Now, shake hands and promise me you're going to deal with it later — peacefully. For now, you're going to put the good of the team first."

Neither boy rushed forward. Dana slid his toe back and forth on the ground. Benton didn't look up.

"My patience is running out," the coach warned.

Then Dana stuck out his hand. Benton followed his lead.

"Good!" said Coach Kingsley. "Now get out there and put some life into this game!"

With a two-goal lead, the Rams were riding high. Even though the Anchors played a tougher game, the Rams still controlled the ball during the start of the second half.

Dana ached to get in on some real action. Too much of his time was spent getting set for plays that never came about. Time and again, a stray ball was the only thing that came his way.

All the time, he wondered whether Benton would keep his part of the coach's deal. Deep down, he doubted it.

And, anyhow, he thought, how can anyone expect me to forgive Benton? My father saved his life — and his sister's — and he turns around and blames him for the fire!

A roar from the crowd pulled his attention toward the Anchors' goal. Their defense was tied up in a battle to hold off a determined Rams offense.

Dana watched anxiously. First the Rams had the ball, then the Anchors, then the Rams.

"Get it out of there, guys!" he yelled. "Come on, Anchors!"

The Anchors dug in. It was worth it.

A Rams wing had worked his way into the clear by a few feet. He rushed forward and booted the ball toward the goal. It wasn't a great kick, but it looked like it was going in.

Jazz lunged after it. For one second, it looked like he wouldn't reach it. But he did. He stopped the ball with his open palm and tipped it in front of the goal line.

Pete Morris swept by and booted the ball the other way. The late afternoon sun blinded Dana for a minute, but then he saw the ball traveling just beyond him.

"Way to go, Jazz! Way to go, Pete!" he shouted

as he ran after it. In the distance, he could hear the Anchors' cheerleaders. They were calling for a double locomotive for Jazz and Pete.

Jack Nguyen got to the ball before Dana. He stopped it, dribbled forward, then passed it over to Lance. It traveled a few more yards toward the goal, then Lance booted it over to Abe.

The Rams targeted the Anchors' left wing. Two tacklers moved in on him from across the field. Abe saw the coming onslaught. He passed the ball crossfield to Benton.

Dana was just a few feet in front of him. A pack of Rams closed in on Benton now. He had to get rid of the ball or lose it to one of the enemy. So he passed it to Steve.

Just like Abe, he could have passed it to me, Dana realized. As he watched Steve go after the ball, a new idea crossed his mind. I bet the Rams have figured it out. They know I'm not going to get the ball. That's why I'm not being covered!

Steve must have made the same discovery. He flicked the ball over to Dana, who was closer to the goal — and open.

Dana caught the ball with his knees. He let it

drop in front of him, then came at it from an angle and booted it to the left side of the goalie.

Score!

The Anchors were finally on the scoreboard, one goal behind the Rams.

Dana felt ten feet tall. He leapt into the air for joy.

"Nice shot, Dana," said Steve, slapping him on the back. A few teammates waved in his direction. Most of them just looked at the scoreboard and cheered.

The goal seemed to have awakened the Rams' defense. They dug in and worked hard to keep the Anchors from scoring another.

Most of Dana's time was spent traveling back and forth across the center line. He stayed alert, waiting for an opportunity to come his way. Once he got a chance to take the ball away from a Rams forward in his territory. But a penalty was called on the other side of the field. The Rams kept the ball in their control.

They took it all the way to the Anchors' goal

area. It looked as though they were set for an easy goal. Louie Ladd was in the clear and kicked the ball toward the far right side of the net. Jazz was way over to the left. There was no way he could stop it.

But out of nowhere, Tucker leapt in front of the ball. It walloped him on the side of the head and sent him reeling. The ball bounced high up into the air, then out of bounds.

"Great save, Tucker!" Dana called to him. "That's using your head!"

There was no reaction from Tucker. He was obviously dazed.

The Anchors' defense was clearly starting to tire. The Rams held on to the ball until they were back in scoring position. All three Rams forwards were in the clear when Sam Mikula, their left wing, took his shot. He feinted Jazz to one side, then booted the ball to the other.

The black-and-white ball sailed across the goal line and into the net.

The scoreboard now read: Rams 3, Anchors 1.

"Come on, you guys," shouted Coach Kingsley. "You can do it! Plenty of time!"

But the clock showed that less than ten minutes remained in the game.

Then, once again, Dana got another opportunity to help the team. He got a pass from Steve, who was running alongside him. They were halfway between the center line and the penalty area. On their left, a Rams fullback was approaching, hoping for an interception. Way to the left, Abe Strom was also running down toward the goal.

As the Rams tackler approached him, Dana passed the ball over to Steve. The tackler shifted direction. Steve flicked the ball back to Dana.

Dana dribbled it a few yards, then half-turned and booted it over to Abe, who was now all by himself.

But the kick was too strong and a little too far to one side. It bypassed Abe and bounced out of bounds.

Instead of setting up a goal, he had blown the Anchors' chances.

Dana could feel the chill blowing toward him from almost the entire team. Across the field, Benton looked as though he was going to shout something mean, but he shook his head and frowned instead.

Dana knew he couldn't let it get him down. If he did, he'd be useless on the field.

Still, he dragged a little as he ran back up the field to get in position for a pass. As he jogged along, just inside the sideline, he heard someone in the stands speak sharply.

"Say, pal, would you mind putting out your cigarette? I have a lung problem. Smoke really bothers me. Okay?"

"Sure," came the answer. "Wish you'd said something sooner. No problem."

The brief conversation made him think of his father. Would Dad have to be extra careful to sit in the "No Smoking" section from now on? he wondered. And what about Benton? How bad are his lungs now? Look at him over there, huffing and puffing.

Benton had slowed down a lot by now. A pass in his direction from Mike went right by him. Dana recovered it and started dribbling it downfield, toward the Rams' goal. Two halfbacks were nearby and went after him. He waited until they were almost on top of him. Then he booted it to Steve, who was running alongside and calling to him.

Here you go, Steve, he thought. It's all yours. It's about time I set you up for a goal.

In a single motion, the Rams' backs turned onto Steve, who flicked the ball over to Lance.

By now the action was well over the center line, moving closer and closer to the goal.

Dana kept up with Steve and Lance as they gradually advanced.

Suddenly Steve slowed down. Dana was about five yards to his right and a few feet behind. The Rams seemed to have forgotten about him — or they were counting him out again.

That was their mistake. Steve half-turned and passed the ball to Dana.

He trapped it with his right shin and stepped on it. Then he drew back a few steps and moved in for the kick. Head down, he drew back his right foot and booted the ball squarely with his instep. There was a thud as the ball made contact with the top of his laces.

The hard, solid kick went right where Dana

wanted it to go — to the wide open space at the left side of the goal.

Score!

The stands went wild, shouting his name. Dana Bellamy, the Anchors' right wing, had just scored his second goal of the game.

The score now read: Rams 3, Anchors 2.

12 • • •

As play resumed, Dana noticed that the other guys weren't so cool to him. Maybe they don't buy all the rotten things Benton's been saying about me, he thought. Or maybe it's just 'cause I'm scoring some goals. I hope they can see I'm not letting him get to me. I'm still doing all I can for the team.

There was no time to brood about his problems. He had to keep up with the ball as it moved back and forth, up and down the field.

With just a few minutes remaining, Paul Crayton stole the ball from a Rams forward, deep in Anchors territory. A quick look around showed that he had a clear field toward the Rams' goal. He got off a solid boot for a breakaway, hoping that one of the Anchors' midfielders or forwards would make it pay off.

For a moment, it looked as though it would — until a Rams tackler stole the ball from under Benton's nose.

The proud possessor of the ball didn't have much time to gloat, however. Dana moved in on him and blocked a flick pass to his left. Steve got the ball on the rebound and started to set up a goal play.

He faked a pass to Dana on his right, then drew back a few steps. He kicked the ball with all his might.

"That sucker's gone!" Dana yelled.

He was right.

The game was now tied: Rams 3, Anchors 3.

The entire team broke out in shouts and cheers. They exchanged both high fives and tens, clapped each other on the shoulders, and danced for joy.

Dana noticed that in the midst of all the hoopla, Benton stayed away from him. He tried to tell himself that it didn't matter, but he knew that deep down it did.

Stunned by the sudden change on the score-board, the Rams dug in. As soon as they got the ball, they moved it right across the center line. Within seconds, they were deep in Anchors territory.

But the Anchors were revved up, too. They pressed as hard as they could — just a little too hard.

As Louie Ladd tried to position himself for a goal attempt, Tucker moved in to steal the ball from him.

Tweeeet!

The referee pointed at Tucker. "Holding!" he announced.

Dana had seen it happen. Tucker had lost his balance and started to slip. He automatically reached for something to keep from falling. It hadn't seemed like an intentional violation, but the ref had decided it was.

"Direct free kick," he called.

This could be the final straw for the Anchors, Dana thought as he saw the Rams get set.

But the kicker was too anxious. The ball was way

too high. It sailed over the goal by about two feet.

Maybe there was still time for the Anchors to win the game after all.

On the coach's signal, Mike Vass got into position for the goal kick. He gave the ball a good wallop downfield, right to Steve. Steve trapped it with his chest, turned, and headed with it toward the Rams' goal. Before he got very far, he was hemmed in by two Rams tacklers.

Abe was nearby, but a swarm of Rams was waiting to descend on him. Dana was in the clear on his right. Steve flicked the ball over to the Anchors' right wing.

Dana caught it on his shin, let it drop, then started dribbling toward the goal. He was just about to kick it when he noticed Benton nearby.

Benton was all by himself. There wasn't a single Ram within ten yards. It was a perfect spot for a goal attempt.

Dana was in a predicament. He could pass it to Benton or go for the goal himself.

He kicked.

Thud!

The minute his toe made contact with the ball,

he knew it was all wrong. The ball went flying too far to the left — and out of bounds.

Benton shot him a look that would have peeled the skin off a crocodile. Dana turned red and looked away from him.

Had he gotten greedy? Or was it Benton? Would he have passed the ball if someone else had been where Benton was? A goal that late in the game could have won it for the Anchors.

To everyone else, it was just a missed goal, but Dana was sure Benton thought it was more than that.

Meanwhile, now that the Rams had control of the ball, they got ready for a final push. A few lucky breaks and a tired Anchors defense worked to their advantage.

With just seconds left to play, Louie Ladd made a "do or die" attempt. Breaking away from a tangle in the center of Anchors territory, he wasted no time. He booted a twenty-yard kick that sent the ball scurrying by Jazz and into the net.

Whistles blew all over the field as the score went up on the board and the game ended.

Rams 4, Anchors 3.

As the two teams trotted off the field, there wasn't much cheering on the Anchors' side. No one had much to say. The members of the team drifted away in groups of two or three. A few straggled off by themselves.

Dana was one of the stragglers.

There was no practice the day after the game. Instead, right after school, Mrs. Bellamy took Dana and Christy over to the hospital.

"Dad, they got you into a chair!" Christy shouted.

Mr. Bellamy laughed. "No, I did it all by myself. I worked on it before you got here and — presto! — here I am."

Dana went over and hugged his father. He was too happy to speak.

Mrs. Bellamy kissed her husband, then asked, "They're releasing you tomorrow?"

"Right. But don't bother coming over before eleven o'clock. That's when the whistle blows and the prisoners make a dash for freedom."

Dana smiled. Mr. Bellamy's good humor was back in full force.

"So, what's new back there? How'd your game go yesterday, Dana?"

Dana told him the sad result.

"But Dana, two goals! Wow! You must have passed Steve Rapids by now," said Mr. Bellamy. "Imagine — top wing, Dana Bellamy," said his father. "Of course," he went on, "that's not what's important — except that it shows you're not giving up just because the team is in a slump. It's times like that when everyone has to pitch in — you, Steve, Benton, and all the guys."

Dana and his mother exchanged questioning looks. Was this the time to tell him about the stories going around? He was bound to find out sooner or later. If he were coming home tomorrow . . .

"Want me to tell him, Mom?" Dana asked.

Mr. Bellamy looked from one to the other. "Tell me what?" he asked. "What's the big secret?"

"Go ahead," said Mrs. Bellamy.

"First of all," Dana said, "the Crawfords are mad because you and Mom didn't go over to their house earlier the night of the fire. They think if you had, you might have smelled smoke or something, and the house wouldn't have burned down."

"But they never asked us to stop in and check on the kids," Mr. Bellamy said. "We didn't know they were going to a wedding."

"I've heard they thought we did know," said Mrs. Bellamy.

"Benton said he told me to tell you, but he didn't," Dana insisted. "I swear. And Steve is a witness."

"No need to swear," said Mr. Bellamy. "We should be able to clear that up."

"Except that Grace Crawford won't take my calls," said Mrs. Bellamy. "She's hiding behind the answering machine."

"And there's more," Dana added.

"More?"

"The Crawfords think it was your fault the fire got started in the first place," Dana said. "Benton said they're convinced that you did a crummy job when you rewired the house. And now that rumor is going around town."

"What!" Mr. Bellamy looked shocked. "The *Crawfords* started this rumor?"

"Well, they haven't taken out an ad in the newspaper," said Mrs. Bellamy. "But almost all the neighbors are talking about it."

"And Letitia doesn't even speak to me in school," said Christy. She thrust out her lower lip in a pout.

"That's nothing compared to how Benton's been acting toward me," said Dana. "Especially during Anchors' games."

Mr. Bellamy's face was flushed with anger. "I just can't believe it," he said. "We've been friends with the Crawfords for so long, ever since they moved next door." He shook his head back and forth.

"Don't get excited, dear," said Mrs. Bellamy.

"But they should know I wouldn't do anything but my best for them," Mr. Bellamy continued. "And I'm not exactly new to electrical work."

"That's what I tried to tell Benton, but he won't even give me the time of day," said Dana.

"Letitia stuck out her tongue at me," said Christy.

"It's just unreal," said Mr. Bellamy. "I saved Benton's life that night — and hers, too."

"That's what makes it all so awful," said Mrs. Bellamy.

As he sat there watching the sadness in his father's face, Dana knew he had to do something. There had to be some way to prove that it wasn't his father's fault.

"If only I could get to Benton," Dana said. "Remind him of all the fun we used to have together — on the soccer field, watching videos, playing cards in his secret hiding place. . . ."

"Secret hiding place?" echoed Mrs. Bellamy.

"Well, it wasn't any big deal," Dana explained. "Benton used to call it that. It was just a little corner of the attic, behind some trunks and boxes."

"So, why'd he call it secret?" Christy asked.

" 'Cause he had this big overstuffed chair and stuff up there he could use when he wanted to be alone. He likes to read up there, and once I saw this metal box with a DO NOT TOUCH sign on it. I guess that's where he kept his lucky key rings and stuff like that."

"Oh yes, I remember seeing that when I was looking over the attic," Mr. Bellamy said. "There's an old fan up there and a few outlets. That's the only part of the house I didn't rewire. The Crawfords insisted that it wasn't necessary, since no one ever spent much time up there, but I did warn them not to plug anything into those outlets.

"Funny thing, though, just a few weeks ago, Mert decided they wanted to have the work done after all. So I went ahead and ordered the parts."

"Did you do the work before the fire happened?" Dana asked.

"No, the parts hadn't come in yet," said Mr. Bellamy.

A tiny light bulb suddenly switched on in Dana's head.

13 • • •

The next morning, with his father coming home later that day, Dana knew he didn't have much time to act. He had to do something to prove the Crawfords were wrong about the fire.

He was no expert, but he knew the Crawfords' house almost as well as his own. He might be able to see something the pros had missed. He had to get in there and check things out — especially up in the attic.

It had been a while since his mother had asked him not to go next door. Surely it was a lot safer now. She wouldn't object to a quick look around — especially since it was so important.

He put on his heavy sneakers with the grooved soles. They'd help keep him on his toes.

He slipped under the yellow plastic tape that

surrounded the house and walked inside the front doorway. There hadn't been a door on it since the fire fighters had pulled it away.

A big piece of the roof was now gone. A rough-edged gap showed where it used to be. He could see the brick chimney that was now all blackened with smoke on the outside.

Dana wandered about the downstairs. Most of the Crawfords' furniture was still there, ruined by the fire and water from the fire hoses.

These terrible sights made him sad. He had shared a lot of good times in this house with Benton and his family.

The staircase to the second floor looked the same as always. Above that, he could make out the entrance to the attic. There was the string that pulled down the folding attic steps. The first time Benton had taken him up there, he was so proud of his "secret hiding place." He remembered the old stand-up radio that Benton had gotten to work, even though the sound was sort of scratchy.

"This is my private hideout," Benton had announced. "Nobody comes up here except me."

Dana started to go up the stairs, but they

wobbled as he took the first step. Some plaster started coming down, too. He decided to have a good look around the downstairs. After all, that was where his father had done a lot of re-wiring.

Bit by bit, he looked at what he could see of the wall outlets and the lighting fixtures. There was nothing that looked like a fire had started around any of them.

They're wrong, he thought. The Crawfords have to be wrong. There isn't a clue that Dad's work started that fire. No way!

"Hi! Anybody there?"

The high-pitched voice startled him. He looked back toward the front hall and saw Andrea McGowan.

"Oh, hi," he said. "Better watch your step. It's a real mess around here."

"I thought I saw someone else come in," she said. "You're the second 'private investigator' who's been nosing around."

"You mean besides the cops? And the insurance people?"

"Right." She pulled her hair back into a ponytail, securing it with a rubber twister.

"Who else has been looking around?"

"Guess," she said. "Bet you an ice cream soda."

"No fair," he said. "It could be anyone. Besides, how do I know you'd tell if I guessed right?"

" 'Cause I can prove it on video."

"Really?"

"Uh-huh. I took a lot of videos after the fire."

"Oh, wow!" said Dana, all excited. "Can I take a look?"

"After you guess," she said, laughing.

"Okay, how about the president of the United States?"

"You owe me an ice cream soda," said Andrea. "Come on, I'll show you the video."

They crossed the street to the McGowan house. Andrea led Dana into the den. It was filled with shelves that held books, records, cassettes, videotapes, models of antique automobiles, sports trophies, and a lot of audio and video equipment. She picked out a tape and stuck it into the VCR. Then she switched on the remote.

After the opening gray "snow," a picture appeared on the TV screen. Dana recognized some of the trees in the McGowans' front yard. Then he saw a squirrel nibbling on an acorn.

"Hey, I remember that," he said. "You took it the day we played the Cottoneers. That was a few days after the fire."

"Right."

The tape showed the McGowans' garden, then more "snow," and then the burnt Crawford house came into view. Andrea had done a really good job. You could see the whole house and all the damage from the outside.

"I took this later that week," she said.

A person came into view from the right side. It looked like a kid, sort of tall, wearing a white T-shirt and a baseball hat with the brim low on his face. He approached the house. Then he paused at the doorway and went inside.

"It's Benton!" Dana said. "I can tell by the way he walks — and I gave him that hat for his birthday last year!"

"Right you are," she said. "Still owe me that ice cream soda, though."

It seemed as though Benton was only in the house for a few seconds before he came back out, just like a Charlie Chaplin movie. He was carrying a small metal box. He tried to cram it into his knapsack, but it wouldn't fit.

"I had the camera off for a little while," Andrea explained. "He was really in there for almost five minutes."

"Oh."

Benton still had the box tucked under his arm. The camera followed him as he stopped by a trash can in front of the house. He lifted the lid and tossed the box into the can. Then he brushed his hands off on his T-shirt, leaving black smudges.

"Hey," said Dana, "I'll bet that was the T-shirt he had in his knapsack the day of the Grizzlies game. That could explain why it smelled like smoke. But what was in that box he threw away?"

Andrea shrugged. "Couldn't read the label, even on the zoom."

Too bad, thought Dana. Still, I wonder . . .

Andrea switched off the tape.

"Thanks a lot, Andrea," Dana said. "I won't forget the bet, I promise. But I sort of have to do something now. I'll buy you the soda later."

He left the McGowan house and dashed across the street. There was the trash can he had just seen on tape. It was in the exact same spot.

He lifted up the battered cover and looked inside.

Empty!

Of course, he thought, groaning. That was a while back. Couldn't expect it to be sitting there just waiting for me.

Once again, Andrea appeared from nowhere.

"I thought this was where you were heading," she said. "Looking for what Benton threw away?"

"Right, even though I think I already know."

"You do? What?"

"I don't think I ought to say until I know for sure," he said.

"Like *some* people?" she asked, nodding toward the Crawford house. "I heard what they're saying about your dad and the fire."

"You don't believe those stories, do you?" he asked.

"Of course not," she said. "Neither do my folks.

Everyone knows your father's a terrific electrician."

"Well, I'm going to make sure no one could possibly think anything else!" Dana said angrily. "And I think I have just about enough evidence to prove . . . well, to prove that those stories are wrong!"

"Calm down," she said. "I just want to know —"

"Andrea, I promise, I'll tell you everything as soon as I'm sure."

"Okay," she said. "Just make sure I get the video rights to the story."

She left him on the curb.

Walking back to his own house, he ran through the bits and pieces of the puzzle. First, Benton "forgetting" to ask him to tell his folks about the wedding. Steve was a witness to that. Then there was the "secret hiding place" and the smoky white T-shirt. And Benton's dodging him in the school yard. The way he acted on the soccer field. The videotape. The mysterious box in the trash can.

There were a few questions he still had to sort out, but he was beginning to form a picture.

14 • • •

Mr. Bellamy arrived home later that day. He was so tired, he stayed in bed in his room. Dana and Christy tiptoed around the house to keep from waking him.

In his own bedroom, after supper and home-work, Dana went over his list of "clues." Once he started to put the pieces together, everything became clear. He was almost ready to blow the whistle and clear up the fire story once and for all.

But staying up late made him drowsy in school the next day. Instead of paying attention to what was going on in class, he slipped in and out of dreamland.

And what wild dreams they were: he was up in the attic of the Crawford house . . . Letitia was dressed up as a bride . . . the fan was going round and round, blowing the wedding veil in Benton's face . . . Benton kept coughing and coughing and coughing . . . until Dana walked in wearing a trench coat, booming "I accuse —!"

A piercing voice interrupted his dream.

"Having a little nap, Dana?" Ms. Doherty, his U.S. history teacher, asked.

"Sorry," Dana murmured. "I was . . . uh . . . just resting my eyes."

"Then perhaps you wouldn't mind answering the question," she said.

"The question?" he asked.

"Yes, the question," she repeated. There was a pause as she studied the deep circles under Dana's eyes. "The question about the Chicago fire of 1871? Can you tell us who or what is generally believed to have been the cause?"

Dana sighed. He was about to admit he had no idea. Then, from the deepest part of his brain, a tiny ray of light opened up. He blurted out, "Mrs. O'Leary's cow!"

"Right," said Ms. Doherty, surprised. The class burst out laughing.

For the rest of the morning, he managed to keep his eyes open. Still, word got around fast. Every now and then, someone he'd pass in the corridor would call out, "Mooooooo!"

By lunchtime, he was glad he could relax for a few minutes without fear of falling asleep or getting heckled.

Dana sat down in the cafeteria next to Steve. They started right off talking about the Rams game for a few minutes.

"Looks like you're the leading scorer on the team now," Steve said. "Congratulations, 'top wing'!"

"I'd rather be the 'bottom wing' and have the team win a few more games," Dana said.

"We're getting closer," Steve said. "Have you straightened out that mess with Benton yet?"

"Not yet," Dana had to admit. "But I'm getting closer."

After lunch, the two of them went outside for some fresh air. They wandered around to the front of the school. On the lawn surrounding the flagpole, dogwood trees and azalea bushes were in bloom. As they sat down on a bench next to a weeping willow whose branches drooped almost to the ground, Steve pointed toward the toolshed.

"Hey, there's Benton now," he said. "Wonder where he's headed." Dana followed Steve's pointing finger.

"That does it!" said Dana, jumping up from the bench.

"Hey, where are you going?" Steve called after him.

"To put the final piece in the puzzle!" Dana shouted back.

He took a shortcut through the bushes.

"Benton! Wait!" he called.

Benton turned and stared at him. "For cryin' out loud, Dana, what do you want?"

"Some answers," said Dana, stepping between him and the toolshed. "Like what you're doing over here."

"It's none of your business," Benton snarled. "Get out of my way. I'm already late for my shop class."

Dana didn't budge. "Shop class?" He looked over his shoulder and pointed. "You're going the wrong way. It's back there."

By the time he turned back, Benton had taken off in another direction, running as fast as he could.

Dana went right after him. He wasn't about to let Benton get away. He had to clear things up once and for all.

Lunch break had ended, and the school grounds were almost deserted.

"Benton!" Dana shouted as he closed the gap between them.

Despite Benton's long legs, he had never been a great distance runner. But he was pumping away now, and it looked like he might just outrun Dana.

Then, suddenly, he stopped. He bent over, putting his hands on his knees. He started to wheeze heavily. It sounded as though he was having trouble sucking air into his lungs.

Dana pulled up next to him.

"That's it, isn't it?" he said, jabbing a finger in Benton's direction. "I know what's going on."

Benton coughed, then sneered at him. "Oh, yeah? Like what?"

"I know why you're breathing so hard and

coughing. I've seen you do it on the soccer field a lot, too," Dana said.

"So I've got a cold. Big deal!" Benton wiped his mouth with the back of his fist.

"Yeah, sure," said Dana. "That's what you want everyone to think. Or that you're still suffering from smoke from the fire. But that's a load of bull. Isn't it?"

Benton started to protest, but the words got caught in his throat. He doubled over again, coughing away.

"That's a cough from smoke inhalation, all right. But I'll bet anything it's not just from the fire," he said quietly. "It's from cigarettes, too, isn't it, Benton? That's where you were heading just now," Dana went on. "You were going to have a quick smoke before going back to class, weren't you?"

"So what are you going to do? Turn me in?" Benton demanded. "Go ahead, prove it."

"Smoking's your business," said Dana. "I don't care if you make yourself sick. But —"

"But what?"

"But you lied about telling me to give my folks

a message about the wedding the night of the fire. You didn't want them to look in on you — because you didn't want to take the chance of getting caught smoking, huh?"

"Maybe I just forgot," mumbled Benton.

"Then why would you lie and say you told me? Because you don't want anyone to know you smoke up there in your secret hiding place."

"All right, what do you want, Dana? True confessions?"

"I want you to tell the truth about what caused the fire!"

Benton was silent.

"My dad had nothing to do with that fire, and you know it. In fact, you know exactly how the fire got started, don't you?"

Benton sucked in a deep breath of air. He shook his head. "No, I don't!" he insisted.

"No? Benton, I've got proof! You know Andrea McGowan, from across the street? Well, she took a video. I saw you on tape going into your house a few days after the fire. And I saw you come out with the metal box from the attic. Now why would you go looking around in that mess for a box only to dump it in the trash can in front of your house!"

"You . . . you found it?"

Dana didn't say a word. He just stared at Benton, eyes blazing with grim determination.

"All right! All right! I'm tired of all the sneaking around," Benton admitted.

"Just tell me what happened," said Dana softly. "I'm pretty sure I've got it figured out, but let me hear your story."

Benton cleared his throat and began.

"My secret hiding place in the attic, you know? I used to go up there when my folks were away. I'd tell Letitia that I was going up there to study or read. And sometimes I did. But most of the time, I'd just sit there and smoke."

"Where'd you get the cigarettes?" Dana asked.

"Oh, those guys who hang out back there." Benton nodded toward the toolshed. "A couple of them are in my shop class. I saw them sneak away early for a smoke one day and . . . well, they dared me to smoke. They said I was afraid to even try. So, I called their bluff — and I got hooked."

"You moron," Dana said.

"Yeah, I know. But I never smoked anywhere

else but over there and in the attic. And I always turned on that fan to blow out the smoke, so no one could smell it. If Letitia got wind of what was going on, well, you know what a big-mouth she is. She'd tell my folks and they'd really tear into me."

"So what happened the night of the fire? You must have been up there lots of times before when your folks were out and mine checked on your house," Dana said.

"No, I never dared to take the chance. But then I heard my father tell yours to go ahead with the rewiring in the attic. I was afraid your dad might find some evidence of my smoking. So I decided I'd better get rid of all my cigarettes. The night my parents were at the wedding was the perfect opportunity. So I didn't tell you to tell your folks that mine were going to be out."

"And then pointed the finger at them!" Dana fumed.

"Well, I was afraid someone might have found out that . . . that I probably caused the fire."

"That's what I thought," said Dana, heaving a deep sigh.

"I only had a few cigarettes left in the attic. But it was hot up there and the noise from the fan was lulling me to sleep. So I just put the last two cigarettes into the metal box and went downstairs to bed. But I don't know, maybe I didn't put the one I was smoking out all the way. And . . . and . . . well, I guess that's what started the fire."

"So that's why you came back for the box. You had to get rid of the evidence."

"Uh-huh. If someone had found it up there, I could have been in a lot of trouble. But after that, my mom said that the insurance people suspected it was an electrical fire. So I figured everything was going to be okay."

"So you started telling everyone it was my father's fault," said Dana.

"Well, it could have been," mumbled Benton.

"Benton, you still can't face up to it, can you? You can't keep spreading rumors to try to get the heat off of you. People just aren't going to buy it."

Benton jammed his toe in the dirt over and over. Then he looked up. "You're right. I'm sorry, Dana — really sorry. I've treated you rotten these past few weeks. I guess I just didn't figure what a mess it would turn into."

Dana couldn't believe it — he felt sorry for Benton. He could tell how painful it was for him to own up to something so awful.

"You have to tell your folks about it, Benton," he said. "You have to tell them everything."

Benton looked over at him. "Will you come with me?"

"Sure," said Dana.

15 • • •

When Mr. and Mrs. Crawford heard Benton's story, they were stunned.

"Smoking! Don't you know what that will do to your health?" Mrs. Crawford cried.

Mr. Crawford was silent. Then he said, "Benton, you know how I feel about what you've just told us. But let's put that aside for a moment. I need you to think back to that night. Tell me, do you remember if you used the attic fan at all?"

"Yes, I . . . I usually turned it on when I was up there," Benton mumbled.

Mr. Crawford shook his head. "I knew I should have told everyone to leave that fan alone. The wiring up there was worn out and faulty. Hayden Bellamy warned us about it."

"Why didn't he fix it when he did the rest of the house?" Mrs. Crawford asked.

"Because I told him not to," said Mr. Crawford. He looked hard at Benton. "I didn't know it was used regularly. But Hayden urged me to reconsider. That's why a few weeks ago I gave him the go-ahead to do the rewiring up there after all. I guess that's when you decided you'd better clear out your 'stash,' Benton."

Benton hung his head as Mr. Crawford continued.

"It seems to me we have our answer about the fire's origins. Benton, is it possible you forgot to turn off the fan that night?"

"I was so sleepy, I don't really remember. But I know I turned it on when . . . when I was smoking. I guess I probably did forget to turn it off."

"It must have shorted out, and a spark must have landed on those old curtains I've been meaning to take down," said Mrs. Crawford sadly. "I shouldn't have put it off for so long."

"We're all partly to blame," sighed Mr. Crawford. "I should have told everyone to keep out of the attic until the rewiring had been done. The only ones who are obviously innocent are the Bellamys."

Suddenly everyone turned to look at Dana.

"Son, I hope you know how sorry we are about all of this," said Mr. Crawford. "Your folks have never been anything but kind to us from the minute we moved in to the house next to yours. I'd better go and talk with them. They deserve an explanation — and an apology."

"I'll come with you," said Mrs. Crawford. "But we have to do something about you, Benton." She pointed a finger at him. "First of all, we're going to get you some counseling about smoking. I only hope you haven't ruined your health completely."

"Yes," said Mr. Crawford. "That's just the beginning. We have a lot to talk about."

Dana was uncomfortable. "Why don't I go and tell my folks you'll be over later?" he suggested.

At the end of the week, the Anchors played their final game, with the Otters. By then, Mr. Bellamy had recovered so much, he was able to join Mrs. Bellamy and Christy in the stands.

Dana could sense a big difference as soon as he ran out on the field. No one turned away from him. No one gave him angry looks. Some of the guys seemed a little ashamed about the way they'd acted and mumbled a few words of apology.

Because Benton was in counseling for his problem, he was allowed to suit up for the game. But Coach Kingsley was so disappointed in him that he kept him on the bench.

The Otters took the kick. For the first few minutes, they controlled the ball. One of their forwards broke away and had the ball just outside the goal area. He booted one a few yards to Jazz's left side.

The Anchors' goalie blocked it with his knee. It rebounded over to Tucker, who dribbled it into the clear. Then he booted it across the center line into Otters territory.

Dana and Steve were closest to that side of the field. They went right after the ball. But an Otter halfback got there first.

He tried to position himself for a pass back to his teammates. Dana wasn't about to let that happen. He placed himself in the way and trapped the pass with his shins. He then flicked it over to Steve, who was a few yards away.

The two forwards passed the ball back and forth, trying to find an opening. Two Otter tacklers were on top of them the whole time.

Finally Dana caught sight of Abe, all by himself a little off to one side. Quickly he passed the ball to Abe, who stopped it with the inside of his left foot.

Instantly the Otter tacklers shifted to him.

Meanwhile, Dana had broken away and run down toward the goal. He caught his breath, as usual, not expecting to see any action for a moment. But Abe shot the ball back to him right way. Dana was so surprised, he almost missed it.

He recovered fast. Trapping the ball with the inside of his right foot, he pushed it forward a few inches, then booted it toward the goal.

The Otters' goalie dived after it. He was a yard away as the ball sailed by him.

Goal!

Dana jumped up with joy. Before he could even lift a fist into the air, he was surrounded by a crush of Anchors.

Even Abe hit him with a high five. Abe had been the lone holdout when word had reached the team about Benton's false stories. Now he was grinning from ear to ear.

"Great shot, Dana," he said. As the crowd around the team's top wing broke up, Abe went on. "Listen, I've been meaning to tell you . . . I was kind of sorry I didn't get elected captain," he said. "And when I saw that Steve was palling around with you and defending you, that really bugged me. But I can see the guys made a good choice. He's a heckuva good captain, setting everyone else up and everything."

"Yeah, but I have you to thank for that assist," said Dana.

"As long as the Anchors keep scoring!" said Abe, racing across the field.

A few minutes later, Mac Reese, who was playing Benton's position, collided with an Otter fullback and landed badly. It looked like he had sprained his ankle. Coach Kingsley hesitated a moment, then signaled Benton to go in at his old position at right half.

The Otters managed to score a goal with only a

few minutes left in the half. Their defense pushed hard and got the ball away from the Anchors, turning it over to their hungry offense. After two unsuccessful attempts at goals, they made a move for a third try. But Pete Morris got in their way. He booted the ball all the way down the field in the other direction.

Benton was all by himself when he caught the ball with his chest. He dribbled it forward with an Otters tackler right on his back. He quickly passed the ball in a direction he hadn't tried in a long time — to Dana.

This time Dana was ready. But he wasn't about to hog the ball. He glanced around and saw someone in the clear, with a better shot at a goal. He quickly booted the ball over to Steve, who sent it zooming into the net.

Score! Anchors 2, Otters 1.

Dana clapped Steve on the back. He stretched out his palm for a high five, but someone beat the Anchors captain to it. Benton was all smiles as he slapped five on Dana.

During the half, while Dana was getting a drink of water, he heard his name called from the stands.

He looked up and saw Andrea, sitting a few rows behind his parents and Christy. In her right hand was her video camera.

"I'm taping the game!" she shouted.

"It's about time!" Dana shouted back at her, grinning.

In the second half, the scoring was all on the Otters' side of the field. Dana assisted Abe with one goal, and Benton came through for the other.

In the final seconds of the game, the Otters made one last try for a goal. Jazz stopped it with his head — and the whistle blew.

It was all over: Anchors 4, Otters 1.

"Four goals by four different players," Coach Kingsley said as the team gathered around. "Now that's what I call teamwork."

The crowd poured out of the stands. Dana could see Mr. and Mrs. Crawford walking side by side with his folks. Christy and Letitia were trailing right behind them.

His father seemed to be telling Mr. Crawford something very serious. When he got closer, he could hear what Mr. Bellamy was saying.

"I don't know what it is, but I have this craving for mashed potatoes."

"I'm hungry, too," Christy announced. Dana and Benton looked at each other and started laughing.

It was good to have things back to normal.

How many of these Matt Christopher sports classics have you read?

❏ Baseball Flyhawk
❏ Baseball Pals
❏ The Basket Counts
❏ Catch That Pass!
❏ Catcher with a Glass Arm
❏ Challenge at Second Base
❏ The Comeback Challenge
❏ The Counterfeit Tackle
❏ The Diamond Champs
❏ Dirt Bike Racer
❏ Dirt Bike Runaway
❏ Face-Off
❏ Football Fugitive
❏ The Fox Steals Home
❏ The Great
   Quarterback Switch
❏ Hard Drive to Short
❏ The Hockey Machine
❏ Ice Magic
❏ Johnny Long Legs
❏ The Kid Who Only
   Hit Homers
❏ Little Lefty
❏ Long Shot for Paul
❏ Long Stretch at First Base

❏ Look Who's Playing
   First Base
❏ Miracle at the Plate
❏ No Arm in Left Field
❏ Pressure Play
❏ Red-Hot Hightops
❏ Return of the
   Home Run Kid
❏ Run, Billy, Run
❏ Shoot for the Hoop
❏ Shortstop from Tokyo
❏ Skateboard Tough
❏ Soccer Halfback
❏ The Submarine Pitch
❏ Supercharged Infield
❏ Tackle Without a Team
❏ Tight End
❏ Too Hot to Handle
❏ Top Wing
❏ Touchdown for Tommy
❏ Tough to Tackle
❏ Undercover Tailback
❏ Wingman on Ice
❏ The Year Mom Won
   the Pennant

All available in paperback from Little, Brown and Company

Join the Matt Christopher Fan Club!

To become an official member of the Matt Christopher Fan Club,
send a business-size (9 1/2" x 4") self-addressed stamped envelope and $1.00 to:

Matt Christopher Fan Club
c/o Little, Brown and Company
34 Beacon Street
Boston, MA 02108